What is Wyrdwood?
https://www.angelmccoy.com/wyrdwood-home/

Dedication

While writing this book, I had to make the decision to help two of my family members—Bobbi Boo and Simon—cross the rainbow bridge. Boo was a sassy tuxedo cat who had been my mini-me for fourteen years. Simon was a loving ginger tabby who had been my mama's boy for thirteen years. That's a long time to have someone in your life.

Boo and Simon were my playmates and my comfort. I could never have predicted how difficult losing them would be. My heart will never be the same.

I dedicate this book and the entire series to these two souls. They loved me and were a source of joy in my daily life. I will miss them until the day I too will cross that bridge and will sleep with them curled up beside me.

I extend this dedication to all the cat-moms and -dads out there who have suffered the loss of a beloved mew. I know your pain.

From Wyrdwood

The Wyrdwood Welcome Trilogy
Stalking the Moon
Jumping the Moon
Hexing the Moon

Standalone Short Works
Nurse Magdaleine
Charlie Darwin and the Trine of 1809

The Kitty Kats Around Series
The Catsitter's Conundrum (2022)

Kitty Kats Around #1

The Catsitter's Conundrum

by Angel Leigh McCoy

Contents

Introduction

MAYOR VIOLET BAGLEY
Documents events.

[Begin incident report.]

A situation has come to my attention. This file contains witness testimonies. I will be employing a Bareface charm to explore events surrounding the crime in question. I must determine whether any breaches of secrecy occurred. Once I've heard all the details, I will make my determination about how to respond.

—Filed with the Wyrdwood Mayor's Office, Violet Bagley

♦♦♦

◆

**Home is where
the cat is.**

—Kitty Kats

◆

1

KITTY

Describes the events of that night.

There was a stranger on my front stoop. His voice squeaked when he talked. He said, "You have until Friday, you know?"

I pulled the door shut and headed down the walkway. He followed me to the sidewalk, undaunted by my cold shoulder.

I'd made it clear by my body language that I wanted nothing to do with him and his narcissistic bowtie. He probably thought he was on the cutting edge of fashion, and I didn't want to be the bearer of bad news.

"Did you hear me, ma'am?" he asked. "You have until Friday."

Ma'am. The most passive-aggressive insult in the English language.

I stopped under a streetlamp and turned to face him, squaring off, chin tucked in tight. "Why are you here?" I glared and stuck my hands to my hips.

He halted before plowing into me, but only just barely. Swaying, he took a step back to keep from toppling.

I waited for his answer. I couldn't believe he'd shown up at my house at dinner time, just to tell me something I already knew. Did he think I'd write him a check on the spot? Did banks do business that way?

"I'm doing you a favor," he said. "You need to understand that your home is on the verge of foreclosure."

"Why you? Why now?"

The question turned his face into a mask of dark shadows. No more Mr. Nice Guy—as if there'd been any true niceness from the start.

He said, voice low, "I wanted to see your reaction."

"My reaction?" A sick feeling churned in my belly. "You wanted to see my reaction when you told me the bank was going to take my home from me—the home I've lived in for thirty-three years?"

"Yes."

"Why?"

"I know who you are. Who your daughter and son-in-law are, and I know what they did. I wanted to witness your family's karma catching up with you."

In my mind, I unhinged my jaw, swallowed him whole, and then belched loudly.

Aloud, I said, "You know one of his victims."

"Uh huh. My mother."

I had no words to reply. Of their own accord, my fingers reached out and brushed down the sleeve of his jacket, perhaps trying to comfort him or let him know that I understood.

He jerked away from me, turned on his heel, and stalked off.

That hurt more than anything else he'd done, unreasonably so. The man—whose name I never actually caught—had been one in a long series of recriminations. I was guilty by association.

No one seemed to understand that I was also a victim of my son-in-law's grift.

I took a deep breath of the savory evening air. Someone had their fireplace going. This would have pleased me if it weren't for the worry suffocating all my joy. If the bank foreclosed on my home, I and my daughter would be homeless. My throat closed up, and my hands shook.

I hadn't thought to grab a jacket. I had chugged out the

front door as soon as I'd seen that bowtie standing on my stoop. I'd pretended I was going for a walk. I didn't want him in my house, judging me.

Because I didn't want to run into him again, I ignored the cold air and just kept walking, pumping my arms as if I could punch away my troubles with each swing. I did psychic violence to my son-in-law with each step.

When I first spotted the dancing orange-red light behind the curtains at the Ortiz residence, it mesmerized me. I stopped and stared for too long, trying to figure out what I was seeing. When the flames slithered up the curtains, I understood. House fires are terrible monsters that start small but grow quickly and consume everything in their path. Like most elements, fire goes about its business with neither judgment nor mercy—until stopped.

I'd never seen a fire so heartbreaking as the one that engulfed the Ortizes' beautiful old Victorian. That house had stood happily for over a hundred years. In my mind, it cried out in pain and fury.

I patted my pockets—no phone. I'd left it at home. Fortunately, another neighbor had called 911.

Sirens filled the neighborhood, echoing off houses, and the fire took over for the sun as it set, lighting the neighborhood.

One moment—that's all it takes for your life to suddenly become unrecognizable.

My husband and I had moved into the neighborhood when we were first married. We'd spent thirty-three years there, raised our daughter there, and then my Bob had died there. As I watched fire devour that house, I felt it like a wound to my world. It may as well have been my own home burning. Metaphorically speaking, my home was burning to the ground, and there seemed to be nothing I could do about it.

Tears welled and flowed down my face. They blurred my vision, twisting the sight of the flames into a bad acid trip. It was all just too much!

Until it wasn't. I come from stoic Oregonian stock, so I mustered, wiped my eyes with my sleeve, and joined two of my neighbors to watch the spectacle. They glanced up as I approached, nodded, and then went back to spectating. The atmosphere was somber.

"I hope everyone got out," I said.

Harut replied, "No." Contrarian by nature, he often confused "yes" and "no."

"No?"

"No stench of burning fat. No one in there." Harut's full name was Harutyan Mushyan. His aralez ancestry—winged dogs—showed in the prominence of his nose. If anyone could smell burning fat, it would be him. He was proudly Armenian, lived three doors down from me, owned a high-end shoe store downtown, and had four children. His wife Bettina stood silently in the circle of his arm. I'd never heard her speak.

"That's a relief." I made a face.

Harut shook his head.

I said, "I'm supposed to catsit tonight for the Garretts. I hope the fire doesn't spread." The Garrett house occupied the lot next door to the Ortizes.

Harut said, "The fire department has it under control."

The Chapman-Silva couple arrived to stand with us.

"What happened?" asked Rose Silva.

I shrugged, "Not sure."

Margo Chapman asked, "Anyone in there?"

"I don't think they were home. Their car's gone." I smiled at the women. In their seventies, they had been in the neighborhood longer than Bob and I had. They were good neighbors, kept their lawn mowed, and only occasionally hosted raucous parties on their backyard deck—Wine & Bridge &

Whine Parties, WBW for short. While Margo was a hundred percent human, Rose had magickal blood. I'd never heard what kin she came from, but the green sparkles in her eyes gave her away despite the cataracts that had begun to thicken there.

Rose commented, stretching her neck to peer around, as if that would help her see better. "I don't see the Ortizes."

"They're not home, sweetheart," said Margo, raising her voice to be heard.

Another neighbor joined us.

"Hey, Mike," Margo greeted the man.

"Hey." Mike Cook waved half-heartedly. To humans, he looked like a large and looming lumberjack. To anyone with magickal blood, he was an orcneas, a bulky race with tusks that protruded from his mouth. Mike had decorated the ends of his tusks with black stone balls that reflected the firelight. The rounded tips made the tusks resemble—a bit shockingly—small arching penises. Whether that had been his intention or not, no one had ever had the nerve to ask him.

Mike had purchased his home in the late eighties and had raised six kids there. His wife, a normal human, needed a wheelchair to get around—a situation completely unrelated to her having birthed six kids.

Mike said, "The old lady sent me out to find out what's happening."

"Fire," Margo replied.

The rest of us nodded in agreement. We stood side-by-side, watching the drama unfold.

The firefighters dragged out their hoses and sprayed giant streams of water at the burning house.

Rose hugged herself. "Please don't let it be arson. That's the last thing we need."

"Their boy is eight now," said Harut. "That's the age."

"What?" I asked. "The age where you burn the house down?"

"Playing with matches." Harut shrugged. "I'm just saying."

Mike didn't take his eyes off the fire. "I bet it's insurance fraud."

Margo put an arm around Rose's shoulders. "They recently sold their boat, you know? Might be they need money."

Rose stuck out a long-nailed finger and pointed at a car parked down the street. "Isn't that Sherrie Abbasi, the girl who babysits for them?"

I followed Rose's finger to the young couple. They were leaning as one entangled unit against a dirty sedan.

Mike said, "By the steamed-up windows on that car, I'd say she and that boyfriend of hers were getting it on."

"Suspicious," said Margo, nose tipped high in the air.

A new fire-department vehicle pulled up to the curb. A man in a sharp uniform got out. He scanned the looky-loos until his attention came to rest on me. He smiled and nodded.

I gave him a small smile and an even smaller wave.

Margo, Rose, Harut, Bettina, and Mike looked back and forth between us.

After a beat, Rose asked, "You know the fire chief?"

"Used to," I replied. "Long time ago." In my mind, I added, Not long enough. The wounds of high school never quite healed nor did the loves. Forty years may have passed, but the man still made my stomach flip every time I saw him. I, of course, had become skilled at ignoring it. I was married.

And then I remembered—I wasn't technically married anymore. Death had done us part.

I dropped my chin as a wave of sadness washed over me. I took a deep breath then immediately regretted it. Smoke from the fire filled my nose. I broke into a series of coughs serious enough that Margo put her hand on my back.

"You okay?"

"Yeah. It's the smoke."

"We should probably go inside," suggested Mike without moving.

No one else moved either.

The fire chief headed for the fire trucks. His name was Elias Kariuki, but everyone called him either Eli or Karaoke (a bastardization of his last name and—unforgivably—one of his favorite pastimes). He preferred Eli. He'd always been cruelly handsome, but in his uniform, with his shaved head and muscular body, he was torture. Why did men age so much better than women?

I had once managed to tolerate the pencil-thin mustache he'd insisted on growing in high school—and still stubbornly wore. He was a Normal, but his physical and mental prowess made up for the lack of magickal blood. When honest with myself, I had to admit that Eli Kariuki was the one who got away.

"Hush," I told myself.

Margo asked, "Excuse me?"

"Nothing." I waved it off and watched Eli stride across the lawn, backlit by the raging fire. The firefighters admired him, it showed, and it put those butterflies back in my belly. For a moment, I was in high school again at the Homecoming beach bonfire, watching Eli laugh and rassle with his buddies. He'd been big even then, a football player; and I'd been a band nerd, flute.

We'd done plenty of rassling ourselves, in the back of his parents' Dodge. My mind suddenly filled with an image of us, our clothing askew, bodies on fire, and the windows so fogged up that the rest of the world ceased to exist.

"Stop it!" I told myself. That was a long time ago.

That time, Margo side-eyed me but didn't say anything.

A loud bang startled us all into jumping. One of the upstairs windows had exploded. The house was beyond saving, but at least the firefighters were keeping the fire from spreading to other homes.

"Well," I said. "I'm going home. My daughter has moved back in."

Margo nodded sagely. "I heard what happened. So sorry."

"I warned her about that man." I shrugged as if to say it was out of my hands, wrapped my arms even tighter around myself, and headed down the street. That man was my son-in-law, and he had killed my husband.

◆◆◆

◆

**If you're not moving fast enough,
The Universe *will* goose you.**

— *ancient satyr saying*

◆

2

DIANA
Is Kitty's adult daughter.

Ice cream—the dinner of the gods. The best thing I had to look forward to that day was ice cream for dinner. I had moved back in—much to my shame—with my mother.

Sitting at the kitchen island with a bowl, a spoon, and a quart of vanilla-caramel-chip ice cream, I scooped a spoonful from the container, bypassed the bowl, and ate it directly.

Apparently, someone's house was on fire. The sirens had woken me from my nap, but I couldn't be bothered to go confirm it.

Mom had run off earlier and was probably exercising her morbid curiosity, gossiping with the neighbors.

Mini-Mimi yipped. She was my teensy Yorkshire terrier. She yipped again.

I looked down to where the dog waited on the floor. "You know the rules. Mom first." I pulled another scoop and proceeded to savor it, making eye contact the whole time.

Mimi whined and squirmed.

"I know," I said. "I probably should've gotten double chocolate fudge. It might've made me feel better." I licked off the spoon. "Next time," I promised myself.

Mimi let out a cry that resembled a baby's.

I peered down at her. "Really? That's how it is? Oh, all right." I put a small spoonful of vanilla ice cream in the bowl, dug out the sneaky chocolate chip and ate it, then moved the bowl to the floor. "Don't snarf it. That's all you're getting."

Mimi had already consumed the ice cream before I'd even finished speaking. The Yorkie-brand vacuum did her best to lick the bowl clean.

I leaned on the counter and saw myself reflected in the microwave door. For the first time in my life, I looked my age—thirty-two. Old.

To avoid myself, I turned my attention to the kitchen at large. I'd grown up there. I had memories of baking cookies with Mom, of learning the family chili recipe from Dad, and of cooking a disastrous boeuf Bourguignon for my first boyfriend when I was sixteen. This was after he took my virginity, and he never showed up for that dinner. I've hated French food ever since.

At thirty-two, I saw the kitchen as shabby. I noted the spaghetti sauce spatter on the wall behind the stove, the worn traffic patterns in the linoleum, and the way the counter-top laminate had chipped and come unglued. It looked like I felt—dulled and abused.

A glance to one side revealed the boxes containing my belongings—everything that mattered and too much that didn't. Like an iceberg, the true extent of my baggage hid under the surface, sitting squarely on my heart.

Three days earlier, a much-appreciated friend had helped to move me in. For the first time in over thirteen years, I returned home—not just to visit, but to stay indefinitely. I had failed at the esteemed institution of marriage.

A fat drop of melted ice cream fell off the spoon. I looked down and noticed the papers lying there, a drip of Heaven on them. I wiped the ice cream up with my finger and said, "Waste not, want not," then stuck it in my mouth.

I stared for a moment at the papers without seeing them. They slowly came into focus, and the top sheet had the word "OVERDUE" printed in red. I picked it up and looked it over. With growing alarm, I stuck the spoon back into the ice cream and examined the entire pile of delinquent bills.

The front door opened and closed. Mom had returned. She appeared in the doorway and stared at the quart of ice cream. "Di," she said. "Your dog pooped in the foyer again. And you're eating ice cream? Did you eat dinner?"

"What is all this?" I asked, holding up the bills.

Mom blinked, confused. Then she crossed to the island with purpose. "Give me those," she ordered. "They're nothing to worry about." She snatched them from me.

"Mom, what's going on? Are you in trouble?"

"The only person in trouble here is you, kiddo. You show up on my doorstep in the middle of the night with your suitcases. Your boxes are cluttering up my dining room. Your dog is pooping in my house. And now you're going through my personal papers? We obviously need to establish some boundaries." Mom clutched the bills to her chest.

"Since when did you and Dad use credit cards?"

"Not me. Your dad. Look, I've got it under control. The estate is going to... His life insurance... It's complicated. Just don't worry, okay? I'm handling it." Mom opened a drawer in the little desk on the far side of the kitchen and stuffed the papers inside.

I said, "You know, I can help you if you need it."

"With what? You don't have a pot to piss in." Mom went to the sink and turned on the water. She didn't, however, do anything with it. Instead, she fisted her hands against the edge of the counter. That meant she was fighting to be patient. I recognized the posture well.

"Seriously, Mom," I said. "I can help."

With her back to me, her voice sounded low and tight, "How about you start by getting a job?"

My hackles prickled. "I'm trying!" My inner teenager raised her ugly head, and Petulance was her name. "It's not my fault no one will hire me!"

A thick silence hung between us, and I imagined my

mom grinding her teeth. Eventually, she said more lightly, "Answer my question. Why are you eating ice cream before dinner—and worse, why's your dog eating ice cream?"

"Because I'm depressed." I gazed down at the container. "Want some?"

"No. I'll be having a healthy meal, thank you very much. Would you like an omelet?"

"Is there bacon and cheddar?"

"Yes."

"Then yes, I'd love an omelet." I dipped into the ice cream one last time and licked the spoon. "How'd the fire turn out?"

"The Ortiz house burned down."

"Aw. I loved that house. Why didn't you take Mimi with you to pee."

"I didn't have time."

"Mm. Anybody hurt?"

"No, thank goodness. It seems no one was home."

I slid off my stool and bent to pick up Mimi's ice cream bowl.

Mimi's tail wagged.

"You're welcome," I whispered and took the bowl to the dishwasher. By the time I returned to my seat, a black cat had leapt up and was licking the ice cream straight out of the container.

"Um, Mom?" I grabbed the tub away from the cat, earning an angry hiss. I recoiled but saved the ice cream.

"What?" Mom had her head in the refrigerator.

"Whose cat is this?"

"What cat?"

♦♦♦

◆

**For the cat is cryptic,
and close to strange things
which men cannot see.
He is the soul of antique Aegyptus,
and bearer of tales
from forgotten cities in Meroe and Ophir.
He is the kin of the jungle's lords,
and heir to the secrets of
hoary and sinister Africa.
The Sphinx is his cousin,
and he speaks her language;
but he is more ancient than the Sphinx,
and remembers that which
she hath forgotten.**

—H.P. Lovecraft, The Cats of Ulthar

◆

3

MUSE
Is the King of Cats.

I walked into the joint like I owned it. The time had come for a change. The Ortiz kid no longer amused me, and his parents were sissies who believed their stuff was important. They kept limiting where I could go, and I knew how that story ended. Eventually, they'd stick me outside and leave me there. No. Hell no. I would not be tossed out like yesterday's trash.

I was a king in exile, and I needed a comfortable bed and an attentive entourage of minions to dote on me. I believed I had found just the right patsy.

I'd always been a no-nonsense kind of guy. Once I'd made up my mind, I didn't stop. My plan worked. The old family was out—scorched earth—and the new family was in.

Only problem, the new family had a dog. I'd encountered it before on my travels around the 'hood. It was a noisy troublemaker with a ridiculous name.

That name—Mini-Mimi—was as pretentious as a name like 'Paris Hilton.' Seriously.

Nevertheless, I felt a certain kinship with the woman called Diana. She had been exiled as well. That, I understood. But while I sympathized with her, I wished she and her dog had gone elsewhere.

I sat at the edge of the counter, looked down at Mini-Mimi—that ragged puff of fluff—and pondered what would happen if I broke its neck. It wouldn't be hard. A few quick shakes. It weighed less than a rat.

I wouldn't actually do it, of course. I was above that. Besides, I knew the hell that would rain down on me if I got caught. I would put up with Mini-Mimi because I coveted a position in the household. Nevertheless, I found no shame in indulging in a little murder fantasy.

I licked around my mouth and tasted the sweet cream lingering on my whiskers. I'd nailed the stealth approach and had gotten in several licks before Diana had discovered me. Score one for me. I prided myself on my thieving abilities—a skill learned by necessity after being dethroned. After all, I was a survivor. A royal scoundrel.

"Well," said the elder human woman, the one they ironically called Kitty. "Who are you? You must have followed me in."

I carefully displayed my tail—my singed tail—on the side where she stood.

"Wait, I recognize you," Kitty said. "Honey, I think this cat belongs to the Ortiz family. Oh, you poor baby." She massaged my shoulders in just the right way, and my motor turned over. I didn't try to stop it. The motor had great power for taming minions.

Diana made a pouty face. "Is she hurt?"

He, I corrected her with my mind.

"I don't think so. Just some singed fur." Kitty leaned in close. "I bet you're hungry, aren't you?"

Diana asked, "Do you think she'd eat dog food?"

He'd. And no. Gross.

Kitty stopped rubbing my neck and moved away. "Lucky for you, kitten, I just bought some cat food to have as a back-up for catsitting."

Diana recoiled. "Catsitting? What does that mean?"

"I'm catsitting for the Garretts. I'm staying at their place tonight. Remember? I told you yesterday."

Diana had forgotten but did a cat-worthy job of pretending she hadn't. "Oh, that's tonight?"

Kitty went to a grocery bag on the counter and took out a mysterious and enchanting can.

"I'd love it if you would move all these boxes down into the basement while I'm gone," Kitty said.

The familiar belch of a cat food can being opened made me salivate. I licked my lips.

Diana said, "I'll move them as soon as you clear Dad's stuff out. It's a freakin' labyrinth down there. I can barely find the bed."

"The Garretts went to Hawaii for their fortieth wedding anniversary." Kitty's diversionary tactics were also impressive.

"It's nice of you to watch their cat while they're gone."

"Well, they're paying me."

"It's a job?"

"They call it a gig, honey. I've joined the 'gig economy.'" She made the quotation-marks gesture.

"I see."

"I know cats. It's a perfect fit, and I need an activity to keep me occupied now that your dad is gone."

Kitty placed a bowl of wet food in front of me, and I was struck deaf to the rest of the conversation. In my mind, I waxed poetic about the gravy. Better, less messy, than mouse. Is savory, yes. Lick every delicious drop, quick!

By the time I'd finished eating, the conversation had shifted.

The older woman asked the younger one, "How's the job search going?"

"Fine. I sent my resume out to a few places yesterday."

"Mm."

"Don't be a Debbie Downer. I'm a great network engineer. I'm marketable."

"I appreciate your confidence. It's a good thing you got your Bachelors."

I left the empty dish for the servants to clean up and looked over the edge of the island. Gauging my trajectory, I leapt and chose to land right beside Mini-Mimi, making her jump and yap. I gave her the ol' side-eye as I walked past her. With head and tail in the air, I left the room to find a quiet, warm spot to take a bath and a nap.

Diana asked, "You letting her stay?"

"I think it's a him," Kitty corrected. She was a woman of extraordinary insight. "What else can I do? He's homeless."

◆◆◆

◆

**Take time to love your neighbors.
You never know when their
security cams will come in handy.**

—from the Wyrdwood Welcome Wagon brochure

4

KITTY
Fends off Greta.

Diana left to walk Mini-Mimi. The instant she was out the door, I pulled the messy stack of bills out of the drawer where I'd stuffed them. I straightened them into a neater pile. The order of the sheets didn't matter. They were all overdue and equally bad. They made my stomach hurt.

My husband, Bob Kats, had worked as a physical education teacher for disabled grade-schoolers. He'd had much more heart than sense, and he'd died with three full credit cards, a double mortgage, and a near-empty bank account.

I, of course, hadn't been aware of any of it. I'd foolishly let Bob handle our finances throughout our thirty-year marriage. He'd done it all from paying the bills to filing our taxes. I'd assumed he was doing a bang-up job. Truth was, he'd been robbing from Peter to pay Paul and driving us straight into financial ruin.

Bob had left me only memories and bills. Even the insurance money hadn't made more than a divot in the balance due. The payout on Bob's teacher pension had kept me from being homeless for a few months, but that was running out, and I had to make some tough decisions.

Bob had always insisted that I not work. After his death, when I figured out I'd need to get a job, I'd taken inventory of my skills. I didn't have many, and those I had belonged to antiquity. The world had moved on from what I'd learned in high-school typing class.

So, I decided to catsit for fun and profit. Financially, it was the equivalent of spitting on a forest fire, but it made me feel productive. Baby steps.

Hugging the paperwork to my chest, I heaved a huge sigh. I had to learn how to handle money, but I panicked when I thought about how I might lose my home, and my mind shut down.

"Tomorrow is soon enough," I said aloud. I went to the bedroom I'd shared with Bob and hid the bills in my dresser, under my underwear. I shut the drawer quietly so as not to awaken mischievous spirits.

The next morning, I tugged my carry-on suitcase out of the closet and began to pack for the overnight catsit. The Garretts had hired me to sleep in their home and care for their cat both morning and evening. I was free to go about my business during the day but would have to return every night until the Garretts came home. It was my first overnighter, and I packed everything I might need: pajamas, a robe, toiletries, and a small flannel throw to put over my pillow—because I tended to drool when I slept. I wanted to leave as little of myself behind as possible.

I walked the block and a half to the Garrett home, pulling my rolling suitcase behind me. Spring had sprung with enthusiasm, and the crocuses were blooming around the Garrett's yard. The house sat on a half-acre lot. It screamed Americana with its pillared front porch, dormer windows, white paint, and flag proudly flying. The trees surrounding it had lived longer than I had and provided beautiful shade in the summer.

The house fit in with all the others within a six-block radius known as the Eastridge neighborhood. Most had been in the same family for generations.

My husband's family—the Kats family—had first arrived

in Wyrdwood in the mid-1800s. When they immigrated, the officials shortened their true name—Katsaros—to Kats, and thus a new branch grew on the family tree. The first Kats ancestors to land on the shore were fleeing persecution. In their Greek village, the eldest son had been accused of murder—and was guilty as sin. The family knew he'd be executed so they fled to America. Yes, I'd married into a family of murderers.

The Katses finally settled on the Oregon coastline in Wyrdwood. They built up a fortune in the lumber industry, and the Katses had been a fixture in town ever since. Bob's great-grandfather had even been mayor.

Through Bob's side of the family, the Katses descended from sphinx kin. Bob had exhibited all the secretive and controlling personality traits one might expect from someone with sphinx blood. Diana had similar traits, although I liked to believe that my dakini ancestry tempered Diana's need to continually test and maintain boundaries.

My earliest ancestors came from Tibet, where dakinis were women who walked the sky. They were complicated beings who wielded both the sweetest and the sharpest feminine powers.

Over the generations, our bloodlines were watered down. Bob and I were mutts, Diana even more so, though that made her no less powerful. We were hybrids of mixed ancestry, unique, just as all beings are.

I carried my suitcase to the front door and used the key the Garretts had given me to let myself in.

"Hello, Greta," I called. "It's your catsitter. I'm here to take care of you." I left the suitcase just inside the front door and headed for the kitchen. A few days earlier when I'd stopped by to pick up the key, Pam Garrett had shown me around, so I knew where to find the cat's dishes.

The Garrett household contained an odd mix of antiques and modern art. I assumed it resulted from a clash between Pam's taste and her husband's. The art on the mahogany-paneled walls included Kandinsky, Picasso, and Budan. Their bright, bold colors rebelled against the traditional crown molding and earth-toned brocade upholstery. On every flat surface, there stood a stone statue. Their flowing surfaces revealed no identifiable shape, and yet they insinuated the human form. Their bends intimated a sensuality that surprised me. In passing, I dared to run my hand down the smooth curve of a wave-like statuette.

The sound of a hiss made me freeze and search around. I found two wide green eyes staring at me from around the corner to the dining room. Miss Greta was a tiny girl, but a brave one. She hissed again.

To her, I was a stranger in her home. Though she'd met me once before, she didn't know me.

"Hi, Greta," I said quietly and gently. "I'm Kitty. I'm going to feed you while your Mom and Dad are gone."

Greta hissed again.

"It's okay." I averted my eyes to avoid challenging her. I set my purse on the floor and slid it softly toward her. "Want to sniff my purse?"

I went to the kitchen counter, half-turning my back on Greta so she'd see I was no threat. Pam, Greta's mom, had left a note on the counter. I stood over it, reading.

> *Hi, Kitty!*
> *My husband, son, and I will have landed in Hawaii by the time you read this. Sunshine and sand! Don't be jealous! I'll bring you back a treat.*
> *Text if you run into any trouble whatsoever, though it may take me a few hours to get back to you. My son has several big meetings with investors, and I'm his assistant.*
> *You can rely on the Ortizes in a pinch. They*

live in the big green-shuttered house next door, as you probably know. They have a copy of our key and can be your backup if you need them.

Also, I forgot to tell you that the Buddhist monk who blesses our house once a month may come by one evening. I've told him you might be there when he arrives. Just let him work his magick, and he'll leave when he's done. I've already paid him, and he has a key.

Oh, and I made a batch of blackberry jam before I left. There's an open jar in the refrigerator and more in the basement if you run out. Help yourself.

Thanks again for taking care of our baby.
Pam

I had texted her, the previous evening, to reassure her about the fire. Pam had not responded. I imagined her busy with her son's business schmoozing.

I dared a glance at Greta. She had her eyes on me, but her nose to my purse. I took it as a good sign, a first step toward winning her confidence.

When I went to grab her dirty food dish off the floor, however, she came rushing toward me, put herself between me and the dish, and hissed vehemently.

I almost laughed. The tiny creature was so fierce! She was adorable, though I doubt that was the impression she'd wanted to make. I swallowed my laughter.

"I'm not stealing your food," I explained. "I promise. I'm going to give you more." I made a slow blink at her, the kitty sign of trust. I showed her by closing my eyes, that I wasn't a predator.

She didn't back down.

I reached for the bowl, and she planted her front feet and hissed again, getting down into a pre-attack pose. I backed off. I wasn't afraid she'd hurt me—too badly—but I didn't want to stress her out any more than I had to.

I went to the cat food cabinet and searched for the treats Pam had shown me. I found them and tossed a few down by my purse. Then, when Greta went to get them, I stole the food bowl. Victory!

◆◆◆

◆

Sharing is caring,
Often daring,
And always airing.

—Kitty Kats

(groan)

— Diana Kats

◆

5

KITTY
Has a near-death experience.

Greta eyed me differently after the treats. She still wasn't sure about me, but she'd stopped hissing.

"That's a good girl," I told her, keeping up a constant one-sided conversation. "Good girl, Greta. Did you like those treats? What a pretty girl."

As I washed the bowl, I glanced out the kitchen window. The fire next door had reduced the proud Victorian to charred skeletal remains. It was an eyesore, at best, and I wondered whether the Ortizes would rebuild or sell the lot.

Fire Chief Eli was still there, and as if he sensed my eyes on him, he looked up.

I ducked down, startled Greta, and had another hiss directed at me. She hadn't liked the sudden movement. *Oops.*

"I'm sorry, pea." I sat cross-legged on the floor to be on her level. "I'm ridiculous."

Greta stared at me, unblinking, from behind the table leg.

I tried the slow blink again then looked away entirely. "You're okay, honey," I told her. An assurance I wished someone would say to me.

The smell of the fire lingered inside the Garretts' home—or in my nose. It was undoubtedly making Greta extra jumpy. Seated on the floor, I stuck a leg out, my sock-covered foot moving toward her.

"Want to smell my foot?" I asked her. Getting a sniff was often the first step toward friendship, and the foot at the end of a long leg would seem safer than my hand.

I kept my eyes averted, coaxing her with gentle admonitions about what a good girl she was. Patience is your friend when dealing with a shy cat.

Eventually, she crept forward and sniffed my foot. "There you go," I said, keeping my voice soft and gentle. "That's me. I'm Kitty, and I'm here to take care of you." I know I sound like a fairy godmother when I talk to cats, but I don't care. It helps them get used to me, and who's to say they don't understand me? I'm rather convinced they do. So, bibbidy-bobbidy-boo to that.

When I didn't move, she sniffed again.

Then I made the mistake of looking directly at her.

She hissed her displeasure and backed away to the table leg.

"Oh, honey," I said. "You don't need to be afraid of me. I'm your friend." But, she *was afraid*.

Once it was clear she wasn't coming out from under the table, I snuck back up to the window and peaked out. Eli had his back to me and was surveying the blackened husk of the Ortizes' house. I resumed the washing of the cat's food dish.

"That charred house, Greta," I said aloud, "is the perfect metaphor for my life right now."

Eli moved out of sight behind the sole-remaining firetruck while several firefighters continued to dig through the rubble. It was Saturday, and a gaggle of local kids on bikes gathered by the curb to watch.

I heard a masculine shout. On the other side of a half-burnt pillar, the firefighters were converging to look at a particular spot. Eli joined them. He leaned over and put his hands on his knees, looking down at whatever it was. One of the others used a shovel to overturn the ash.

My stomach dropped uncomfortably. "Oh, no," I said aloud. "What did they find?"

I dried my hands on a towel and headed for the door.

Before I could even question the wisdom of it, I was crossing the lawn.

One of the firefighters lifted his nose into the air then tilted his head to listen. His gaze slid over to me, and he stood up straight, suddenly hard-focused on me. He tapped Eli's bicep, pointed me out to him, and said something I couldn't hear.

Eli straightened, put his hands on his hips, and then suddenly—quite suddenly—his eyes grew wide and he started running toward me.

I stopped, confused.

He was waving his arm wildly.

I looked around.

"Back up!" Eli shouted.

I didn't understand until a loud crack split the air. I looked up.

In the next moment, Eli scooped me off my feet and slung me over his shoulder in a fire-fighter's carry. He didn't even stop running. With every bounce, I had my breath knocked out of me.

Behind Eli, right where I'd been standing, a large tree limb came crashing down. It was singed and blackened. The fire must have made it brittle. The explosive crack I'd heard had been it breaking off the tree.

I hit Eli on the lower back as soon as he slowed down enough that I didn't need to cling with two handfuls of his jacket.

"Stop! Put me down!"

He stopped and turned in place, looking back at the thick limb. His arm around my thighs was strong and surprisingly warm.

"Put me down!"

He waved his free arm at the other firefighters. "Get this damn area cordoned off! Now!" He was panting and hugging my thighs like his life depended on it.

"Eli," I said, trying to sound stern.

Almost to himself, he said, "You could have been seriously hurt."

"But I wasn't. You saved me. Thank you. Now put. Me. Down." My blood was pooling in my head. I pressed my hands against his lower back to raise my torso up a bit and to stop the tremble that had started in me at the thought that I might have been injured, if not killed.

"It's good to see you, Kitten." That had been his nickname for me in high school. It softened me to hear it and brought me closer to aftermath tears. I sniffed to fight the buzz in my nose.

Eli turned around again so he could see the Garrett's house. "I thought you lived down the street. Did you move?"

"I haven't moved. Put me down."

"I saw you carry a suitcase in there."

"Not that it's any of your business," I said, "but I'm cat-sitting. Okay?" I smacked him on the rump. "Elias Michael Kariuki," I said with my mom-voice. "Put me down right now or I will scream."

I felt his body shake though I couldn't hear his laughter. He gently slid me back across his shoulder and set my feet on the ground. He didn't let go until I was stable.

"Thank you," I said, mostly for setting me down but also for saving my life.

"You look good," Eli said, checking me out. "I heard about your husband. I'm so sorry."

I gave him a sideways glance. *You look good, sorry your husband's dead.* That was an interesting train of thought.

I brushed myself off, even though I wasn't dirty. "What did you find?" I asked, back on track.

Eli ignored my question and counter-asked, "I don't suppose you know where the Ortizes are?"

"No. You haven't found them? You don't think they're in..." I indicated the burnt-out husk.

"No. Everyone who was there got out. Even the cat."

"But you can't reach them?"

"Not yet. They're not answering their cellphones. Catsitting, huh?"

"And you're sure they're not...in there?"

"Positive. The cadaver dog came up empty."

"You said someone was there? Who?"

"Babysitter and the Ortizes' eight-year-old son."

I studied the man's face. His features were so familiar, even after all those years, and as I looked at him, I had the overwhelming urge to lean against him. It made my nose tickle again and nearly brought tears to my eyes. It was a feeling of such intense loneliness that it briefly overwhelmed me. I knew in my heart that it had nothing to do with Eli and everything to do with Bob. I missed his physical presence in my life.

Eagle-eyed Eli studied me.

I moved to a position between him and the Ortiz house, putting my back to him. "Wh-what caused it?"

"Candle. Pretty sure. The fire spread outward from the dining room. Speaking of which, I'd love to take you to dinner sometime. So we can, you know, catch up. Reminisce about old times."

I froze. "Dinner?"

"Just friends," said Eli. "Nothing fancy. I've been dying to try that new Swill-n-Grill bar down on Delaney Road. What do you say? Tomorrow night?"

I was shaking my head even before I answered, "I have to catsit."

"Some other time, eh?" Eli moved to where he could see my face, and I his.

I peered at him through narrowed eyes and replied, "We'll see."

"Good." Eli's smile always got the corners of my mouth turning upward. "I'll talk to you soon," he said and would have walked away if I hadn't had more questions.

"Hey," I said. "Do you think it was arson?"

Eli considered his words. "We're not sure. We want to talk to the kid before we make a call. We figure he's with his parents. Once we find them, we'll get more answers."

"So what were you all looking at over there? What'd they find?"

Eli appeared to debate whether he should answer or not, kicking at a chunk of burned wood on the lawn. Finally, he looked up and teased, "Wouldn't you like to know?" Then, he turned and walked away.

I followed, hurrying to stay on his heels.

"C'mon, Eli, you can tell me."

After a few more strides, he stopped. "One of the guys found the Ortizes' safe. It was under the floor in their bedroom, it seems. And before you ask, no, I have no idea what's in it." He waved his index finger at me.

Undaunted, I asked, "You don't think the Ortizes did it, do you? Insurance fraud?"

Eli laughed, and his eyes sparkled. "I'd forgotten how earnest you can be. I doubt it, unless they also intended to put their child at risk. But it's one of the theories we're investigating." He put his hand over his heart. "Anything else, Madam Interrogator?"

"No." I shook my head small and tight. Earnest? I didn't know whether to blush from insult or from pleasure. Either way, I blushed.

I thought Eli noticed, and that made me blush even more.

"Chief!" called a man. It was Manny Ortiz, Gregorio Ortiz's younger brother. Thirty-something, he had the look of a CEO on the way to a merger. He crossed the trampled lawn with large strides, his suit-coat flapping. "Chief! I need to talk to you."

"How can I help you?" Eli asked, his expression gone

completely neutral, though he took in every little detail of the man's bespoke attire, hundred-dollar haircut, and soot-caked fancy shoes.

The man led with his hand, offering it to shake, and stopped when he was within reach. "My name is Manny Ortiz. I'm Gregorio's brother. I got a call this morning saying there'd been a fire and that my brother was unreachable. Can you tell me what's going on, please?" He was out of breath—more likely from concern rather than from the speed-walk across the yard.

Eli shook the man's hand. "Mr. Ortiz, we haven't been able to reach your brother or his wife to inform them of the fire. Have you spoken with them?"

"No. I assumed they'd be here. What happened?"

"Not sure yet. The forensics team says someone purposefully shut off the electricity to the house then used force to get in through the side door. We found broken glass inside. We don't know what happened after that, but we found evidence that the fire started in the dining room, probably with a candle."

I stared at Eli with my mouth open and upper lip quirked. He'd only told me a fraction of that.

"I see," said Manny Ortiz, frowning. "Was anyone in the house?"

"We believe your nephew was, but you don't need to worry. We believe he got out. We found no victims."

"I tried both my brother's and my sister-in-law's cells this morning, soon as I heard. I got voicemail for both of them." Manny turned around to face the house, hands on hips. "Damn it. That house has been in our family for generations."

Eli moved to stand beside him. "I'm sorry for your loss."

"Can I go in? See what can be salvaged?"

"I'm afraid not yet. Besides, I doubt you're gonna find much worth salvaging. Between the smoke damage, the water damage, and the fire itself, it's pretty much totaled. Not to mention dangerous."

I stepped up to join them, putting Manny between Eli and me. "I'm sorry this happened, Manny. I can only imagine what it's like to lose your childhood home like that."

Manny looked down at me, and I gave him my most sympathetic expression. I'd known Manny all his life. I remembered the blue balloons hung on the front gate when he was born, and what he'd looked like learning to ride a bike and, years later, riding his skateboard up the street. I'd attended his father's then his mother's funerals. We'd been neighbors, which in my mind made us practically family.

"Thanks, Mrs. Kats," Manny said. "It's not just a house going up in flames, it's memories."

"No, dear," I told him. "Nothing can destroy your memories. You hang on to those."

He smiled with sad nostalgia, and I wondered whether he was married. He and Diana would make a lovely couple. I checked his hand. No ringy dingy.

A red convertible pulled up in front of the house and a woman leapt out of it. She immediately began screaming, "Oh my god," over and over. It was Badahlia Ortiz. Her husband, Gregorio, emerged slothlike from the driver's side, staring with his mouth open. They were both dressed in fancy evening attire, disheveled on the morning after a long night on the town.

My heart ached for the woman's anguish. Poor thing. What a terrible way to learn you've lost everything.

Gregorio moved to support his wife, but a strange pallor had come over his tanned face. He looked waxen.

Manny and Eli took off toward the Ortizes.

I followed, of course.

Gregorio spotted his brother and pointed an accusing finger at him. "Did you do this? This better not be a result of one of your pranks!"

Lifting his hands to indicate his innocence, Manny said, "My pranks don't burn down houses. Wasn't me, brother. I was too fond of our—now lost—family fortune."

Turning his attention to the fire chief, Gregorio said, "My son was here last night."

Under his breath, Manny commented, "Ten to one, he's the firestarter." Only I heard him. I pretended to ignore it.

Badahlia was melting. She shouted at Eli, "Where is my son?"

◆

**Home is
where you dance
(and fart)
without shame.**

—attributed to Bob Kats, post-mortem

◆

6

MUSE
Observes from a safe distance.

My whiskers twitched in disgust. I didn't like Manny Ortiz. He smelled unnatural. Perfumed. What was he hiding under all those layers of scent?

My perch on the Garrett's porch offered me a clear view of the unfolding drama, well away from falling tree limbs. Kitty's near miss had startled me. I liked her hands way too much to lose her so soon.

My previous caretakers were throwing a hissy fit. They hadn't found the brat. Like me, they didn't trust Manny. They pointed fingers at him and asked him what he'd done.

Manny—little man—pretended he was innocent. "I just got here," he said. "I didn't have anything to do with this."

"Where's Antony?" Mama Badahlia had always pronounced her son's name with a hard "tuh" instead of a "thuh." Most everyone else, including his sire, called him Andy. I called him The Brat.

Manny answered, "How should I know? We assumed he was with you."

"No! We left him with the babysitter. Are you sure..."

"Ma'am," said the burly chieftain. "We're sure. There were no victims. We spoke with Miss Abbasi. She believes your boy walked to a friend's house."

"Believes?" Papa Gregorio's neck turned red. "Have you searched for him?"

"Only in the rubble, Mr. Ortiz. And I assure you, he's not

there. We assumed he was with you and your wife."

Badahlia was keening again. The pitch of it made my back teeth ache.

The chief was out of his depth. The mama frightened him.

"Mister and Mrs. Ortiz," Kitty said. "I'll mobilize the neighbors. We can search the area. If he's injured or unconscious somewhere, we'll find him."

"Injured?" Badahlia squeaked between wails.

"Eli, you'd better call the sheriff," Kitty said. She was level-headed. I'd chosen well.

Badahlia collapsed against Gregorio. The chieftain stepped away with his cellphone. And Kitty headed off down the street toward her den.

Manny Ortiz stood there like a dog without an owner, doing nothing. Eyes vacant. After a long pause—too long— he followed Kitty.

I followed *him*. I zigged and zagged through the bushes, detoured around the old wheel-barrel planter, slid under a car, and darted across the street. I was faster than him, so I had to stop and wait a few times. I used my favorite hiding places to watch him.

Manny walked with his hands in his pockets, another reason I didn't trust him. Show me your paws, little man, so I can see whether your claws are in or out.

◆◆◆

7

DIANA
Almost gives up, then lightning strikes.

Unemployment. The place where intelligent people go to die. My mother doesn't understand how hard it is to find a good job. She never had to work. My generation has very different challenges from what hers has had. I suppose I should be grateful she isn't pushing me to find another husband to "take care of me." We all know how the first one worked out. He—Kyle—had wanted me to get pregnant and quit my job. I almost gave in, but my intuition fought the idea. I procrastinated it, and thank God I did. Shortly after the truth came out about what he'd done, my old job fired me.

"Miss Kats," said the owner of a local hardware store where I was interviewing to clerk. "I'm afraid you're not right for the position."

"Not right?" I said. "In what way? I'm overqualified for this position. Please. I'll sweep floors. I'll clean the bathrooms. I'll stock shelves!"

The owner shook his head. "Don't make me say it, Miss Kats. We value our customers, and..."

And they would not react well if they saw me working there. He didn't have to say it.

My will to fight drained out of me, and I left.

"I'm sorry," he called after me. Unfortunately, "sorry" doesn't pay the bills. It's damn depressing to live in a town where your reputation has been blown, where everyone knows you, and where they're unlikely to forget that your "darling" husband cheated so many people out of their life savings. At least no one has thrown tomatoes at me. Or eaten my face. Both are distinct possibilities when you piss off the residents of Wyrdwood.

I needed a job. I couldn't live with my mother forever. My plan was to save up enough to buy a little house of my own. A cute cottage with a fenced yard, a little garden, and big sunny windows. Mini-Mimi and I could live there happily for the rest of our lives.

What I wanted more than anything was stability. My soon-to-be-ex had systematically destroyed the world I'd built. His name was Kyle Butts. I'd refused to take his last name, even hyphenated with my own. Can you imagine? Diana Kats-Butts? No. On reflection, that may have been the beginning of all our troubles. We'd only been married for five years when the FBI raided our home. For years, my "darling" husband had been scamming the elderly, pretending to be a mortgage consultant. They'd uncovered a brand-new Tesla bought by his "company" and a mansion where he'd entertained his marks.

I'd had no idea what he was up to. *Honest.*

As it turned out, the jackass ended up in prison. The government liquidated all his assets to pay his debt to the people he scammed—and that included both the mansion and the house we lived in. It had been in his family for generations.

I was forced to move back in with my mom.

Fortunately, they didn't throw me in jail too. I spent all my personal savings on a lawyer and was able to prove I was not involved. That was the one up-side to my husband being so sneaky and greedy. He had managed to keep me out of it entirely. He hadn't even bought me any over-the-top birthday, anniversary, or Christmas gifts, the turd.

I can't even imagine what would have happened if I'd had a kid. Poor peanut probably would have ended up in foster care. Thank God we never had children.

Nevertheless, my world was broken. I got depressed, stopped going to work, and lost my job. Fired. Shit icing on a shit layer cake.

So, I'm thirty two and living off my mother. If you'd told me that's where I would end up, I'd have laughed in your face. Yet, here I am.

I hit all the job-search sites on the Internet and found only one that might be a good fit for me—working for the Wyrdwood sheriff's department. Blah. That place was a sucking black hole, run by the village idiot—Sheriff Metzger.

Frank Metzger had won the election because of a joke. Someone ran an ad in the Wyrdwood Gazette inciting people to vote for Frank because it would be funny. It showed an old picture of him dressed as a pink and white bunny rabbit—probably an Easter memory. He was turned to the side, and it was clear that he hadn't been able to zip the suit up because of his enormous belly. Enough of Wyrdwood's residents had voted for him on a lark to actually get him elected. That was Wyrdwood in a nutshell. It was full of smartasses. I'm sure most people thought no one else would vote for him—and voila! We got four years of an innocent human—unaware of magick—as our head of law enforcement.

Needless to say, Mayor Violet Bagley was not amused and has had to take up the slack when it comes to policing the kith community. I have no idea how she's managed to keep poor Frank in the dark about magick or why she hasn't just read him in. Whatever. Not my decision.

One thing was for certain—the police department would know my history. I was desperate, however, and figured I may as well give it one more shot before I took a job doing phone sex.

I summoned the courage to call the main line and got the emergency dispatcher.

"Wyrdwood Sheriff's Department. Is this an emergency?"

"No. Not an emergency." I enunciated extra sharply to ensure she heard right.

"How can I help you, dear?"

"I'm calling about the job opening in your I.T. department."

"About what?" The woman sounded surprised.

"Um, the network specialist job?"

"Don't hang up. One second. I'll patch you through to the office."

"Thank you."

Five minutes later, I had an interview scheduled for that afternoon. They hadn't even asked if I had a degree, so I didn't have to lie.

I was in Mom's dining room, digging through one of my suitcases for a professional outfit to wear, when Mom burst through the front door. She left the door open, and a few seconds after that, a man followed her in.

Manny Ortiz. The crush. From when I was thirteen—the age when I first noticed that Manny was more than just another kid. Manny had been in the same grade as me, and we'd been neighbors all my life. I still remembered him at five years old, running down our street, wearing only—and I do mean *only*—his red cowboy boots. He'd always been the one who was just out of my league.

In the halcyon days of summer break, I'd spent countless hours watching him play basketball in his driveway, wash his parents' cars, and mow the lawn. I'd positioned myself on the front porch swing—the best vantage point—and had pretended to read while my hormones surged. Those were the days.

I stood slowly. "What's going on?"

Mom was already in the kitchen.

Manny answered, "My nephew is missing. Your mother's going to call all the neighbors and find out if anyone has seen him. We're going to form a search party. You want to help?"

I blinked at him. The Ortiz kid was missing? That was terrible, but...I had a job interview. I said, "Later, I will. I have an appointment."

"Ah," Manny said and headed for the kitchen, basically dismissing me.

"It's important," I called after him, defensive, palms upturned.

He didn't seem to hear me.

Mom was already on the phone, summoning her neighborhood cronies.

I continued searching for an outfit.

◆◆◆

◆

**Sometimes, all you need is a
(choose one)
_ Bubble bath
_ Sabbath
_ Sunbath
_ Bloodbath**

—Quiz published in the Wyrdwood Gazette

◆

8

KITTY
Calls out the neighborhood brigade.

When I walked into the house, Diana was—of course—throwing clothes all over the dining room. I couldn't even deal with that. I kept my eye on the prize: the neighborhood contact list attached by the dentist-office magnet to the fridge. I pulled it down and began making the calls.

"Something has to be done," I said.

"That poor boy is out there somewhere, all by himself!" I said.

"He could be hurt! Dying!" I said.

Everyone wanted to help. Bless their hearts.

We arranged to rendezvous in thirty minutes for a quick briefing and route assignment. After the last call, I sat down at my computer and printed out multiple copies of a neighborhood map. By the time I was done, I'd created a five-petaled flower diagram with the Ortiz house at the center.

Manny followed me around, watching. He couldn't help, though he offered several times. Some jobs are one-woman jobs. None of it took long, and thirty minutes later, I was waiting on the front porch, wearing my walking shoes and raincoat—just in case.

Diana came out of the house. "Mom," she said, shaking the spare set of car keys at me. "I need your car. I have a job interview." She looked so grown up in her slacks and blouse. She was even carrying a purse instead of her usual backpack. And, she was wearing makeup!

"Doing what? Where?" My attention was split. The neighbors were converging on our house.

She replied, "The sheriff's department needs a network specialist."

Dubious, I asked, "Are you sure they understand what that means?"

"I hope so. If not, then I'll ask for more money." Diana smiled. I'd seen the expression so rarely of late that I was struck by her prettiness.

"Good luck, darling," I said, watching her navigate the front stairs and the swarm of neighbors. She was wearing high heels!

My cell phone rang. Expecting it to be one of the neighbors I'd left a message for, I just looked at the screen. It was Pam Garrett—Greta's mom. I poked Manny in the shoulder. "Fill them in, would you? I need to take this." When I was sure he'd heard me, I put the phone to my ear and went back inside.

"Hi, Pam. How's it going?"

"Kitty! It's Pam. I'm here in Waikiki. That's Hawaii."

"That's great, Pam." I rolled my eyes. "How's it going?"

"It is so beautiful here, Kitty. You would not believe it. The sun feels so marvelous. You can smell the ocean everywhere you go, and the fooooood! Don't even get me started on the food, Kitty. We attended a luau on our hotel's patio last night, and they had this pulled pork dish that was to die for! Honestly, if I could convince my husband to leave his stupid Poker buddies, I'd retire here in a heartbeat! Maybe I can poison him and get away with it. What do you think?"

"Sounds amazing. Did you get my text? About the fire?"

"Oh, yes! How awful. I'm so glad everyone was okay. No sparks on our roof, I hope?"

"No. Your house is fine. Fire's out."

"Good. I would hate it if Terrance had to fly all the way home just for that. I'd stay here, of course. The hotel is paid for, after all. No reason we should all suffer."

"Of course not."

"You should take a vacation here, Kitty. Today, we're taking a bus tour of a pineapple farm, and, tomorrow, we're going on a sunset dinner cruise with our son, soon as he lands. He had to take a later flight because of work. His business is just booming, you know? It makes me so proud. Oh, I don't mean to brag. How's Diana? Has she moved back in yet?"

A headache stirred behind my eyes. "I have to go, Pam. The Ortiz boy is missing. We're all out searching for him."

"Oh, dear me! Well, good luck finding him. He's a bit of a pissant, that one, but I wouldn't want him hurt. Text me if you need anything. Is Greta missing me too much?"

"Greta? A bit, yes. But she's fine."

Oh, heck! Poor little Greta! I'd forgotten to feed her.

Once the neighbors were all on their way, I made a quick detour to feed Greta. She greeted me with the same hostility as before, but I didn't have time to indulge her.

"Baby," I said. "There's a little boy missing. Let me find him, and then we can get to know each other. In the meantime, I'm going to give you your breakfast, and I need you to stay in your corner."

She was not in the mood for excuses. She placed herself in the kitchen doorway and wouldn't let me pass.

"C'mon, kitten," I said. "Aren't you hungry?"

Greta hissed. She, of course, remembered me as the person who had stolen her food dishes and then left.

When I took a step forward, she lunged toward me, letting me know she'd attack if I tried that again. I retreated. "I don't have time for this, Greta." I closed my eyes and took a deep breath. I had three choices. I could wait her out. I could barge through her and take the scratches. Or, I could leave and let her be hungry. I didn't like any of those options. I just wanted her to be a good girl.

"Why can't you be a good girl?" I asked. "Why does everything have to be a fight? Why does it...so...hard?"

Tears welled in my eyes. My throat tightened, and a sob forced its way out of me. I covered my face with my hands. The pain, the frustration, and the fear I'd been pushing down inside myself finally broke through my barriers. They overwhelmed me, and I couldn't help but cry. My legs weakened, and I sat down on the floor.

"Oh, Greta," I sobbed. If Bob weren't already dead, I'd have killed him. I was so angry and sad that he'd left me in such a precarious position. I'd relied on him, and he'd done the one thing that would ensure my devastation. He'd had the gall to die.

I don't know how long I sat there steeped in my own misery, but I eventually pulled myself together, wiped my eyes, blew my nose, and looked up to find Greta watching me with wide eyes.

"Sweet little warrior kitten," I said. "You win." I stuck my leg out, offering my foot for her to sniff. The neighborhood was looking for Anthony. I could take a moment to coax a scared baby girl into letting me feed her.

Greta inched toward my foot, and I held my breath. If she attacked, I'd suffer the consequences. She didn't. Instead, she took a sniff and looked at me.

I blinked slowly then dropped my gaze.

Greta slinked away, though she didn't take her eyes off me. She returned to her spot behind the table leg and licked her tongue out at me. That meant she was hungry.

I took the win. "Thank you, honey," I said. "I'll get you some breakfast." Food was indeed the great equalizer. For the first time, I had hope that I could win her over.

♦♦♦

◆

**You don't have
To be a fairy
To see magick.**

—Diana Kats

◆

9

DIANA
Takes an unexpected test.

Butterflies churned in my belly. I parallel parked on the street outside the police station, and sat there, waiting until ten minutes before the interview. I checked and double-checked my make-up in the rearview mirror, read over my résumé, and practiced what I'd say.

"Hi. I'm Diana Kats. I'm here to interview... I have an appointment for a job interview. For the network engineer position. Hi! My name's Diana Kats, K. A. T. S. I'm here for the network engineer job. Do I have a degree? Well, I have a ton of experience. I know computer systems inside and out, specifically network infrastructure and security. I've set up and maintained databases, and I can troubleshoot to get to the bottom of any problem." I looked myself in the eyes. "You sound smart. Let's hope that's enough."

The alarm on my phone chimed. It was time.

I opened my car door to get out.

A car horn blasted right in my ear. With a gasp, I pulled the door shut again.

A banged-up Toyota sedan swerved, nearly taking off my door and scaring the hell out of the poor driver coming the other direction.

I saw the Toyota's occupant in profile as he cruised by. He was handsome with a big nose, and strong jaw, just like I like. A little older than me, I figured. He glanced over at me. Eye candy, yes. I watched him go, my head turning to keep him in sight.

He swung his car in to the curb in front of me and parked.

I checked that it was clear then got out. I stepped onto the sidewalk and headed for the station.

"Hey," the driver of the Toyota called from behind me.

I didn't look back. The last thing I needed was a fight with an indignant asshole right before my interview.

He repeated, louder, "Hey!" He slammed his door shut, and the alarm beeped.

I kept walking then heard footsteps running up behind me. I sighed and stopped, resigned to a confrontation. I turned to face him, tipped my head, and gave him a dry look. "Look, sorry. No harm, no foul. Okay?"

I fully expected him to man-splain to me why I should have looked in my mirror before opening my car door, but he surprised me.

"You Diane Kats?"

I blinked, and it took a second before I replied, "It's Di-anUH, like the goddess."

"That's great," he said and grabbed me by the wrist. "Come on." He pulled me toward the police station.

"Hey! Whoa! What's happening right now? What are you doing? Let me go!" I didn't resist too hard. We were, after all, going into the police station. It occurred to me to wonder if opening your car door into traffic was against the law. Did he intend to file a complaint? Reckless door opening?

Much to my surprise, he said, "I'm your new boss." He held the door open, let go of my wrist, and directed me in ahead of him. "Your interview is less of an interview and more of a test. I've got a problem I need you to fix."

What was I supposed to do with that? I mumbled something like, "Ummm, okay."

My new boss led me through the station. It brought back bad memories that I couldn't ignore. We passed the administrative area, the holding cells, the officer locker room, the sheriff's office, and a closed door labeled, "Interview Room."

I pointed to it, "Ummmm..." He blew on by. Not that kind of interview, and he had no sense of humor.

Eventually, we arrived at his destination. He used a keypad to unlock the security door and directed me inside. I stepped into the previous decade. The equipment in the data center couldn't have been younger than ten years old. Their rack cabinet looked like it had spent years in a kindergarten class, the stickers and dents on it revealing its age. Exposed wires ran up to the ceiling then out through a hole in the wall to the rest of the station.

"Oh," I said. I was being diplomatic.

My new boss—whose name I still didn't know—pointed at a white board. "There's the list of problems. Fix the top one, and you've got the job. Then, you can start on the others."

"Number one," I read aloud. "No internet. No sweat." I waited for more. When he just watched me, I asked, "So, I should just..."

"Yeah," he answered as if it were the most obvious thing in the world. "We're stuck here. I've got cases that are languishing because we can't send emails much less access the state databases." He became animated. "Lives are at stake, okay? Work your magick!"

I clacked my back teeth together and shook myself into motion. I sought out the router. The device that connected all the station's computers topped my checklist. As it turned out, it had an error light flashing. I pushed the button to turn it off. While I counted to thirty in my head, I watched my soon-to-be boss.

He had positioned himself at the door and was looking out through the crack. He was dressed in business-casual, a pair of jeans, a plaid shirt, and a blazer, all in shades of blue. He'd recently had a haircut, so it was short and neat. He wore glasses, trendy ones with clear frames and a slight blue tint to the lenses for computer use. I figured him for a wine snob who preferred international film festivals over baseball games. In other words, not my kinda guy.

28...29...30. I turned the router back on. It cycled through its startup routine. As soon as I saw the green light come on, I put myself between it and my new boss. I leaned over it and pretended to examine it more closely. "Hm-mmm," I commented. "Ah, yes. I see."

"Can you fix it?" he asked.

"I believe so. Give me just a second to calibrate the WAN settings and adjust the connectors." I fake-fiddled with the plugs.

I felt him come up behind me, his presence weighty.

I said, "And voila!" I turned to face him and found he was right there, practically on top of me. He smelled so good.

"It's fixed?" He wasn't paying attention to me. He was looking at the router.

"I think so," I said, breath tight. "We just need to test it to make sure. Why don't you go log into your computer and see if you can send an email now."

"Great," he said and strode out.

I exhaled and followed him at a distance. As he bent over his computer, others around the room turned their attention to him, on pins and needles, and when he said, "Yes! It's working!" a general cheer exploded. After that, the sound of keyboards clacking was deafening.

My new boss sat down and checked his email. I stood nearby, twiddling my thumbs.

Just as I was about to start whistling a little tune, one of the deputies rushed over.

"Nick," he said, pronouncing it to rhyme with 'Eek!' "We called the kid's friends. Dead silence in the water. Nobody seen him, or if they did, they're not saying. The neighbors search and trample evidence. They can't found him yet either. What you think's happened?"

My new boss—whose name was apparently Nick—chewed his lip then said, "Either the parents took him, or someone else did."

I had to hide a smile and a widening of my eyes. Nick was a genius!

The deputy nodded sagely. "You have a plan."

Nick stood. "Did you talk to the sheriff?"

"No. He's fishing." The deputy looked over at me. "Fishing for criminals. All the criminals."

Nick glanced at me briefly then said, "Okay then. Call the hospital and the kid's school. I'll put out an AMBER Alert. Let's find out if anyone has seen him. Better get Josie in here, since Auntie's on vacation. Jerry won't be able to handle a tsunami of calls."

"I will do." The deputy walked quickly away like a kid trying hard not to run.

Nick waved me over and said, "You're hired. Talk to Jerry at the front desk. He'll get you the right paperwork to fill out."

"When do I start?"

"Right now. We've got a missing child. We're going to need those computers working. You can use the server room as your office."

The server room. The dusty one with no windows. "Can't I use that desk?" I asked, pointing to an empty one by the window. "I need good light to see all the tiny components."

"Sure," he replied without missing a beat.

Encouraged, I said, "I'm also going to need two flat monitors and a high-speed laptop. The one in the server room is older than I am."

"Okay. Jerry can requisition them for you."

"And as for salary, I need—"

"You'll need to speak with Jerry about that too. He handles all salary issues."

"Okay," I said, turning away. Then I remembered. "Hey,"

I said.

He was halfway down to sitting in his chair, attention on his monitor. He stood back up. "What?"

"Is there coffee here somewhere, Boss?"

He blinked, then smiled. "Yeah, if you want to call it that. Break room's down that hall, just past the restrooms."

"Thanks." I tipped my head in a sort of salute then went to find Jerry and get that paperwork filled out before anyone could change their mind—including me.

♦♦♦

♦

**Ignorant people think
it is the noise which fighting cats make
that is so aggravating,
but it ain't so;
it is the sickening grammar that they use.**

—Mark Twain

♦

10

MUSE
Returns to the business of food.

Well, shiver me whiskers. Divers searched the lagoon for the brat. Kitty stayed out all day, walking around the neighborhood, calling his name until she was hoarse. No sign of him. Finally, she hobbled back to the other house, the one with the fussy kitten. I snuck in with her. She was too tired to notice.

I was starving. Diana had reappeared at dusk, fed her rat, but didn't feed me. No one had fed me since that morning. No way I was going to eat dog food, so when I followed Kitty to the other house, I ate that kitten's food. Greta was too fat anyway.

Don't look at me like that. I left her a few scraps in the bottom of the bowl.

After—finally—filling my belly, I lay down to take a nap with my new minion. Kitty was already snoring by the time I curled up next to her. She was warm and smelled like fresh air and salt. I was going to like having her in my pride.

◆◆◆

◆

**When in doubt or embarrassed,
lick something.**

—bumper sticker with outline of a cat

◆

11

KITTY
Returns to the business of Bob.

At about midnight, I woke up with a stiff neck and a cat in the crook of my arm. I extricated myself, stumbled toward the bathroom, stubbed my toe on unfamiliar furniture—not sure what—and collapsed on the toilet. I was sore and exhausted. I hadn't walked that much in over ten years, and to no avail. That poor little Ortiz boy was still missing.

The search had quickly progressed to a more serious level, with an AMBER Alert and a dredging of the reservoir. My heart hurt with worry for the kid, but we neighbors had done all we could. We'd covered every square inch of the surrounding area.

I took a shower, put on my pajamas, then added more kibble to Greta's bowl. She was extra hungry for some reason. She'd emptied the dish. I chalked it up to anxiety because her parents were gone.

Yawning, I stood at the bay window in the living room and looked out at the neighborhood. I'd lived there for so long, I couldn't imagine going anywhere else. It simply wasn't part of my reality. And yet, my mortgage was in crisis, and getting foreclosed on was a distinct possibility. I didn't know what I was going to do. Bob had spent his retirement fund, and I had none.

The idea that I might end up homeless made my stomach churn. The Tannenbaums had hoisted a tent in their front yard, for their kids to play in. I found myself studying it, evaluating whether it would be a good choice for me when the time came.

I supposed I could live in my car. Lots of folks did it. I felt grateful that Bob had bought an SUV. I could probably sleep in the back.

I compared the cars parked in driveways and on the street from a new perspective. None of those people would ever have to live in theirs. Of course, six months ago, I'd have laughed if you'd told me *I* might have to.

The vehicles on the block were all so familiar—except that one. A nondescript black sedan sat in the darkest portion of the street, between two street lamps. I could just make out a person moving in the front seat, or maybe it was a shadow from the wind-ruffled trees.

A shiver ran up my spine, and suddenly, I felt cold. I told myself that one of the neighbors probably had family visiting.

Nevertheless, I double-checked all the locks before retiring to the Garretts' guest room.

Instead of collapsing on top of the bed, as I had earlier, I got under the covers like a civilized person. It felt like I was at a hotel. The sheets were newer—and nicer—than those I had at home, and they smelled of lavender. It was relaxing and, before I knew it, I was asleep again.

The next morning dawned bright and beautiful. Sunshine streamed in through the windows, and for a moment, I forgot my troubles. I rolled toward the light and came face to face with black fur, a little pink nose, bright green eyes, impressive eyebrows, and long tickly whiskers. He blinked slowly. I blinked slowly back. He was definitely not Greta.

"What are *you* doing here?" I asked the Ortizes' cat.

The cat rolled onto his back and offered me his tummy.

"Good answer." I gave him the obligatory pets. "You must have followed me in, hm? Don't worry. We'll find your human brother and then you can go home to your family. I'm sure they miss you."

The cat rubbed his face on my hand, demanding more adoration. I obliged.

"Are you hungry, honey? Let's get up and have some breakfast."

I set out two bowls of cat food while brewing my coffee. One for the Ortizes' cat and one for Greta—who observed the activities from a puddle of sun on the dining room rug.

The neighbor cat ran straight to the food and ate with gusto. I made a mental note to find out what his name was.

'Round about 8:00 a.m.—after I'd finished the catsitting chores—I returned home. I walked in the front door to find that Mimi had pooped in the foyer again. It was becoming a habit whenever Diana failed to take her out in the middle of the night. I cleaned it up, though technically, I should have made Diana do it. Mimi was *her* dog, after all, and how would she learn if I didn't let her clean up her own messes. Still, I couldn't just leave it there.

Instead—to be helpful, of course—I took my old travel alarm clock out of the closet and set it for 2:00 a.m.

Diana was in the upstairs shower, so I made myself a bolstering cup of tea and checked my phone for news of the Ortiz boy. Nothing. The neighborhood and I had done all we could to help find him. It was in the hands of the police, and so I found myself with no reason not to face my demon—a demon named Bob.

I headed down into my own personal underworld. Diana was right: I needed to sort Bob's detritis. I'd put it off long enough. For six months, I'd been boxing his belongings up, willy nilly, and putting them in the basement. "For later," I'd told myself. Well, "later" had come.

First things first, I set the alarm clock under the guest bed—Diana's bed. That would get her up to take her dog out.

The Ortizes' cat followed on my heels. That poor creature was clinging to me like a lost infant. He and I had that in common, I supposed. He'd lost his loved ones. I'd lost mine. I spent extra time petting him while I considered which box to open first.

I was normally better at organizing. I barely remembered boxing it up. Grief can do that to you—disconnect you from reality. You go on autopilot and, if you're lucky, you don't crash and burn. When you finally do land, you're a stranger in a strange land—to quote a memorable Heinlein title.

Several of the boxes were marked "Clothes," and I just set those aside for the thrift store. I'd get Diana to carry them back upstairs for me. No point in overtaxing myself. One of the benefits of advancing age is that you can use it as an excuse to avoid physical labor.

"Three boxes done," I told the black cat. I opened the nearest one to me. It held Bob's bathroom stuff, shaver, brush, bottles of man-scented shampoo, aftershave, deodorant, and shaving cream. I'd just thrown them all in. "I suppose I should dump some of this stuff out and recycle the bottles, hm? Or maybe there's a homeless shelter that needs them." I pondered. "Or, maybe one of the neighbors could use it." The prospect seemed daunting. "Later," I decided. "I'll figure that out later." I set the box by the stairs.

"Bob was a good man," I told the cat. "I doubt you ever met him, but you would have liked him. Everyone liked him. He could charm the deadliest snake." I opened another box. It contained the clutter that had been in his desk.

"Bob was a dreamer. I've tried to be mad at him for leaving me with all this debt. Five credit cards, kitten. Five. All maxed out. And a double mortgage on the house. I know you don't know what any of that means, but trust me, it's bad. It's like having a pit bull move in next door and, at any moment, it could jump the fence and eat you."

The cat let out a little mew.

"Exactly," I replied. "He gave me a good life, though, while he was here. We were happy and well-situated for retirement—or so he led me to believe. If only he'd told me what was going on, I could've gotten a job. I could've helped." I lowered my voice, "Don't tell anyone, but they're threatening to take the house."

I held a pair of Bob's well-worn penny loafers in my hands. They were Bob. Bob had been a well-worn pair of penny loafers, the kind that are so comfortable you just keep wearing them long after the stitching has frayed.

On impulse, I threw them at the wall. They made a loud bang then rebounded and bounced in different directions, ricocheting off boxes.

I stood there for a moment, still as a rock.

The cat rubbed my ankle and purred.

I took a breath then bent to pet him. "I guess I am mad."

"Mom? You okay?" Diana started down the basement stairs with her dog right behind her. She wore a fuzzy blue robe and had one of my best towels wrapped around her head.

"Yeah. I'm fine. Just cleaning up your dad's shit."

"I got a job," Diana said. She picked Mimi up, kissed her on the head, and put her down on the bed. Mimi ran in circles.

My eyebrows rose in surprise. "Well done, honey! That didn't take long."

"It was serendipity."

"Where? What will you be doing?"

Drying her hair with a towel, Diana said, "At the Sheriff's Department. My official title is Network Specialist. They need someone to manage their computer systems." She moved away from me.

"Wow. Now, aren't you glad you got that degree! I'm so proud of you! When do you start?" I chased her to give her a hug.

"I already started," Diana said to my shoulder. "They needed someone so badly, they hired me on the spot. Benefits are good. The salary's okay—though not what I wanted. The receptionist-slash-H.R. guy wouldn't let me ask for more than he was making. Go figure." She stepped back from the hug and wove through the boxes to the head of the bed. "I have to get dressed. I have to be there at 9:00."

"Don't mind me," I told her. "I'm on a roll."

"I'm proud of *you,* Mom. Going through Dad's stuff. I'll be back this evening, and I can help you."

"Thanks, honey. Any idea what time you'll be back?"

"No." Diana pulled clothes out of her suitcase and shook them out. "We're trying to find the Ortiz kid, and it's all hands on deck until we do. The Ortizes have offered a reward, so the station is being inundated with calls and emails from people claiming to have seen him."

I was reminded of the little girl she'd once been—dressing herself for the first time and refusing my help. It brought a smile to my face.

"Mom. Stop watching me get dressed." She said this without looking up. She knew me that well.

"Sorry, honey. I'm not looking—anymore. How much is the reward?"

"Ten thousand dollars. Must be hard to put a value on your son's life."

"Ten. Thousand. Dollars?"

"Yeah. Ten thousand dollars."

"Ten *thousand* dollars?"

"Yeah."

The cat began purring again.

◆◆◆

♦

**All creatures great and small
have three things in common.
We are born,
We die,
And we like pie.**

—Ginger Fan, owner of the Mousehole Café

♦

12

KITTY
Thinks about the reward.

Breakfast was a tradition in our home, and I loved cooking for Diana. If she were left to her own devices, she'd eat chips and candy for every meal. I scrambled eggs with onions and toasted a bagel for her. While I was at it, I put a peanut-butter and jelly sandwich and carrot slivers into a small paper bag for her lunch. I made a mental note to buy bread, cheese slices, mustard, and bologna—Diana's favorite sandwich.

"Ten thousand dollars," I told the cat, who had followed me back upstairs. "It wouldn't solve *all* my problems, but it sure would help. If only I could be the one to find the boy."

Mini-Mimi came hippity-hopping up the stairs with Diana right behind dressed in khaki slacks and a cream-colored button-down shirt.

"Is that what you're going to wear?" I asked her.

"Why? What's wrong with this?"

"It's just so...beige."

Diana pulled a face and took a stool at the counter where I'd set out her silverware and a glass of water. "Mom. I'm a network specialist, not an exotic dancer."

"I know, I know. It's just that you won't stand out much dressed in that."

"Well, that's the goal. I'm the shadow looking over their shoulders and making sure their computers are working."

"Ah." I set a plate of food in front of her. "Bon appétit," I said with cheer.

"Thanks, Mom. You're the best."

"You're welcome, honey." I stood in front of the sink to wash the pan. "I was wondering."

"Mm-hm?" Diana replied with a mouth full of eggs.

"Do you know Sherrie Abbasi?"

"Who?"

"The Ortizes' babysitter."

"Oh." Diana took a sip of her water. "Why would I know her?"

"Because you're young."

"She's in high school, isn't she? Not everyone under thirty knows each other."

"Well, I've been thinking. If anyone has information about what happened to little Andy, it'd be her."

"I suppose that's true," Diana replied. She glanced at the clock. "I have to go. Thanks for breakfast, Ma. You can just leave the dishes. I'll wash them when I get home."

I rolled my eyes. She knew damn well I wouldn't let them sit that long.

She grabbed her purse and jacket from where she'd left them draped on a box of her belongings.

I met her at the front door with her lunch sack. "Don't forget your lunch, honey."

Diana stared at the bag, then at me, then at the bag again. "You made me lunch?"

"Yes," I said. "You forget to eat when you're working. It's nothing special. Just a sandwich and some carrots." I thrust the bag in her direction.

Diana took it with her thumb and index finger, as if it had cooties. "Thanks. But you didn't have to do that."

"You're welcome." I turned away. "Have a good day!"

With Diana gone, I washed the breakfast dishes then stood at the top of the basement stairs, planning to go down and continue sorting through Bob's belongings.

I couldn't bring myself to move any further.

Then, I heard a revving engine outside, and it was the perfect distraction. I knew the sound. It was the Ortizes' red convertible. It had the kind of engine roar intended to draw attention.

I hurried to the front door and watched them drive by, heading toward their house—or what was left of it. I grabbed a sweater and my keys, and I took off after them, speed-walking. I waved at Margo as I scooted by and called, "No time to chat, sweetie!"

She smiled and resumed pruning her roses.

By the time I caught up with the Ortizes, they were picking their way around the outskirts of the ruins. The lawn was still muddy from all the water sprayed on the fire, and so, they were focused on where they stepped.

"Good morning!" I called.

They both turned to look at me.

I asked, "Has there been any news?"

They shook their heads, and their misery showed on their faces. It didn't look like they'd slept much.

"I'm so sorry," I said. "We looked all over the neighborhood yesterday. If he was injured, we'd have found him. I'm sure of it."

They nodded.

"I heard," I said, "that you've offered a reward?"

Gregorio answered, "Yes. Ten thousand dollars for any information that leads to us finding him. First come, first served, of course."

"Mm," I replied, trying not to seem too interested. Then, a thought occurred to me. I said, "Oh! I've been meaning to tell you. I have your cat. He's fine." When they didn't comment, I continued, "I'm happy to take care of him while you figure out what you're going to do."

"Thank you," said Gregorio.

"What's his name, by the way?"

"We call him Ralph."

"Ralph?"

Gregorio said without humor, "He's a puker. Eats too much then ralphs it up."

"I see."

"When we first got him, the adoption agency said his name was Muse."

"Good to know."

Badahlia had already turned away and was examining the wreckage. Gregorio obviously wanted to do the same.

"Can I ask?" I said, taking a step toward him. My shoe sank into mud, and I shifted my weight. "Can I get the phone number for your babysitter?"

"Sherrie? You need a babysitter?"

"Kind of."

Gregorio took out his phone and poked through his records. He held the display out to me and I copied her info into my phone. As if on cue, a fat raindrop landed on my hand.

Badahlia said, "Greg, the top's down." She didn't move.

I barely managed to get the last of Sherry's number before he took off for the convertible. I followed more slowly. No way I was going to stay behind with Badahlia. She scared me.

"Just out of curiosity," I said as I caught up. "How would one claim the reward, if one had information?"

Gregorio locked down the convertible's roof. "The police are handling that. Do you know something?" His dark eyes settled on me.

"Not yet," I said. The rain poured down in earnest, ending our conversation. I jogged for the closest shelter, the Garrett's house.

◆◆◆

13

MUSE
Shelters from the rain.

Rain is Mother Nature's way of putting a damper on shenanigans.

I didn't let the Ortizes see me. Even if they found the brat, I had no intention of moving back in with them. I ran ahead to Greta's house and, when she got there, I followed Kitty inside. Ever the gentleman, I sat on the foyer rug and cleaned my wet fur. Kitty paused to shake herself off too and spotted me.

"So they called you Ralph, hm?" she said.

That wasn't worthy of a reply.

She said, "That's a terrible name."

I did not disagree. It was one of a multitude of reasons why I hated the Ortizes.

Kitty bent to pet my head. "I'm going to call you Muse. What do you think?"

I dipped my cheek into her palm.

◆◆◆

◆

Yes, You are Magickal Too

*—title of a beloved children's book
written by Wyrdwood author Maggie Flatbottom*

◆

14

KITTY
Hunts down clues.

"If you get this message, help!" The voice of a teen girl came through the cellphone. I froze, shocked.

"Save me!" she continued. "They're torturing me! I'm being held prisoner against my will in high school." Her tone dropped to conversational, "Or, I'm just busy. Spill the tea. Call ya back."

It took me a moment to remember why I'd called. "Sherrie," I said. "This is Kitty Kats. I'm a friend of the Ortiz family, and I wanted to talk to you about a possible gig. Call me when you get a chance." I recited my number, then hung up. My plan was to hire her to help me haul boxes to the thrift store. That way, I could find out what she knows about the fire and the missing boy.

"All in good time," I said aloud, pushing down my frustration at having to wait for her to call back. I was itchy with the urge to discover a clue to the boy's location. The idea of getting that reward made me salivate. I had a knack for finding missing cats, so why not find a missing boy? The principle was the same.

I paced in the Garrett's living room. Muse leapt up onto an armchair to observe. Greta watched me from under the armchair. She still wouldn't let me near her, but at least she'd stopped menacing me. She seemed to have understood that I was the food lady. I bent to take a picture of her then texted it to Pamela Garrett. I typed in a quick report on how Greta was doing, ending with several cat-related emojis and "All is well."

Cat-moms worried about their babies, so a photo and a report went a long way toward easing their minds. I figured she was probably busy because she was in Hawaii and because she had business to attend to for her son, but she could check the text when she had a chance. As someone who remembers what it was like before cellphones, I am lavishly grateful for them.

I tapped my phone against my front teeth, and pondered aloud, "Where could he be, Muse? He's not at a friend's house. He wasn't trapped in the fire. Could someone have taken him? A pervert? A woman who can't have children of her own? They could've seen an opportunity and taken it. Maybe they set the fire to cover their tracks?" I looked at Muse for answers, but he just tilted his head.

"Obviously," I said, as if he'd actually answered me, which of course he hadn't.

Who else might have information about what happened? The answer popped up immediately. The spa. It was a magical black hole that sucked in gossip from all over town. I held out a hand to study my unkempt nails and ragged cuticles—catsitting was rough on the paws. The time had come for some upkeep.

The spa was off the beaten path, a block east of the Oregon Coast Highway, away from the tourist area. It was part of a tiny strip mall with three businesses: the spa itself, a shop that sold new and used musical instruments, and an exotic-meat butcher.

Half-hidden behind a long row of cedar and pine trees, it was strategically located to remain unnoticed by visiting tourists.

On the other side of the highway, several of Wyrdwood's most popular hotels and quaint B&Bs invited tourists in. The Oregon Coast attracted many tourists, and despite

Wyrdwood's attempts to repel them, it was a losing battle. The current mayor, Mayor Violet Bagley, had thrown in the towel. If she couldn't keep the tourists out, she'd herd them away from locals and cater to their needs. Several fancy restaurants, campsites, and beaches occupied the same general area. Locals knew it was all for tourists, but tourists thought they were getting authentic Wyrdwood.

The Bloom and Groom Spa, on the other hand, was for locals. Occasionally, a tourist would wander in, but it was rare. The men and women who worked at the Bloom—as it was nicknamed—had magickal blood or were Normals who knew about the kith. Neither clients nor the employees censored their conversations or hid their magickal abilities.

I'd been getting my mani-pedis and haircuts there for decades. I had attended Olive Crane's retirement party when she'd finally handed her scissors—and the business— to her daughter. Bloom and Groom was a fixture in Wyrdwood. They didn't advertise or hang a sign outside because they didn't have to. Word of mouth spread about where they were and what they did.

The Cranes, both Olive and her daughter June, were of dryad ancestry, so stepping inside the spa was like entering a forest clearing. Sunlight streamed in through skylights and lit the large room with its rays. The floor was a bed of river rocks locked in concrete to create the illusion of nature. Every surface had a plant, and trees in pots stood along the walls. A decorative fountain overflowed into a basin, adding the soft sound of water to the background. It smelled of flowers and forest.

Walk-ins were welcomed. As soon as you entered, a clerk greeted you to find out which services you wanted. I told the green-haired young woman that I'd like a manicure. She asked if I required a private room, and I declined. I wanted the public room, the one where the gossip happened.

She handed me a pair of bamboo-soled slippers—standard procedure for all clients—and I placed my shoes in a cubby hole on the rack. The public room was just beyond the reception desk. Hair-cutting stations lined one wall while pedicure chairs lined the other. Down the center of the room, manicure tables alternated with overstuffed armchairs for customers to relax in while waiting for their nails to dry. The decor was designed to create a casual and pampering atmosphere.

The clientele were a mix of men and women, getting haircuts, shaves, nails trimmed, horns polished, hooves cleaned, and eyebrows plucked.

The clerk directed me to one of the armchairs to wait for a manicurist. "It might be five or ten minutes," she warned. "I apologize for the wait."

"No worries at all," I replied. "I'm in no hurry." And I wasn't. Already, the gossip was rebounding around me, drawing me in. I settled into the chair, closed my eyes, and opened my ears to the conversations.

I heard about money troubles, boss trouble, kid trouble, and lover trouble. I heard about upcoming and recent vacations, about home renovations, and weight-loss failures. None of it was useful.

When my manicurist came to get me, he asked, "Kitty?"

I nodded.

He picked up one of my hands and examined it. "Baby, what are you doing to your hands?" He sounded shocked.

"Catsitting," I replied. "I wash my hands a hundred times a day."

He gave me a scolding look and guided me to my feet. "I have some lotion you can use that will protect your poor abused skin."

I followed him to one of the manicure tables.

"My name's Jacques," he said with a smile. "Let's get you soaking."

"Nice to meet you," I replied.

Jacques was short by most people's standards and small boned. He had the look of a vegetarian or a vegan. His clothes were natural linen, a tunic and loose pants. He wore his black hair in cornrows.

Once I was seated across from him at the small table, he picked up my hands one at a time and set my fingertips in a bowl of soapy water. He gave each a little caress as he did so. "What kind of soap are you using when you wash your hands?"

"Dish soap, usually," I told him. "Whatever's convenient where I'm catsitting."

"I see. You know that dish soap is designed to strip away oil?"

"I know."

"Mm. Just something to think about. Your hands look ten years older than you do."

I shrugged. "Needs must."

Jacques grunted. "This catsitting, is it your job?"

"For now. I use it to make ends meet, so to speak. People hire me to watch over their cats while they go on vacation or business trips. I have a website at KittyKatsAround.com. If you know of anyone who needs a catsitter, send them my way."

"I'm more of a dog person, but I have friends. You should leave a business card. We can put it up on the board."

By "dog," I presumed he meant chihuahuas, poodles, or greyhounds—any of which would have fit his demeanor.

"That'd be great. I don't have business cards yet, but I will. Thanks."

The manicure proceeded as normal. After soaking, Jacques put lotion on my hands and massaged them. I couldn't say a word during this. It felt too good. I owed it to him to honor the experience with respectful silence.

Afterward, he began the nail cleaning and trimming. My cuticles were a mess, a fact he graciously avoided commenting on.

After a while, I asked, "Did you hear about the fire up in the Eastridge neighborhood?"

"I did!" he replied, becoming animated at the prospect of gossip. "Do you live up there?"

"Yes. I was there when the house burned down. Not in the house, but outside. It was a three-alarm fire."

"I heard the house was totaled."

"I'm afraid so. Terrible. Just terrible."

Other ears around the room had perked up. An elderly woman with blue-gray hair said, "The night it burned, I saw the owners."

"Oh, really?" I replied.

"Oh yes. The wife—Badahlia Ortiz—was wearing this over-the-top evening gown. She and her husband were having dinner at the Whitecap."

"What color?" asked Jacques.

"What color what?" the elderly woman replied.

"What color was the dress?"

"Oh! Red as a blood moon. It had bead-work on the decolletage. Very showy for a woman her age. I could practically see her nipples."

"Well, she is a diva," commented the elderly woman's hairdresser wrapping her hair onto curlers. "And she's not that old, Brenda. I'm older than she is."

The elderly woman conceded, "She had lovely breasts."

Having lit the fuse, I sat back and let the information fly.

Another client said, "I heard they were fighting at the Whitecap."

"They were!" replied the elderly woman. "As a matter of fact, he stormed out and left her there to finish her meal—and get drunk—alone. I was embarrassed for her. She was sauced by the time my husband and I were done eating."

I piped up. "What time was that?"

"Oh, around eleven or so. My husband is Spanish. We

eat late."

Jacques wanted to know, "What were they fighting about?"

The elderly woman sat up a little straighter. "Now don't quote me on this, but my impression was that he's having an affair, and she called him out on it. There's divorce in their future."

"Divorce?" said another hairdresser. "That seems extreme. If I got divorced every time my husband cheated, I'd be Zsa Zsa Gabor. Men! Am I right?"

The elderly woman raised her index finger. "I heard Badahlia say that if he wanted a divorce, she'd give him a divorce he'd never forget."

The conversation started to diverge, so I interjected, "I heard their little boy is missing."

Several others had heard the same. Those who hadn't were shocked and concerned. Many offered thoughts and prayers for the boy's safe recovery.

June Crane waved her scissors in the air and said in a wispy voice, "I gave Andy Ortiz his first haircut. He's been coming here all his life. Last time he was in, with his mother, he acted out. I felt a strong vibe of anger coming from him."

Jacques said, "He probably knows his parents are splitting up."

"Divorce is hardest on the children," said another client.

"Speaking of divorce," someone else said. "Did you hear they're closing the Northside dog park next week? To do landscaping."

Jacques' eyebrows jumped.

Someone else spoke what we were all thinking, "What does that have to do with divorce?"

The energy broke back up into pods then, each person speaking only to their cosmetologist. I watched Jacques repair my hands, but my mind was on the Ortizes. It was starting to make more sense that little Anthony had run away.

Maybe even that *he* set the fire and then ran away.

"Or maybe," Diana suggested when I called to tell her what I learned, "Gregorio left the restaurant and headed home to set the place on fire. He has no alibi now. Did you think of that?"

I considered it, then asked, "Why? Why would he do that?"

"So his wife couldn't get the house in the divorce. Out of spite. Plain ol' meanness."

"No, that makes no sense. That house has been in Gregorio's family for generations. I don't think Badahlia could get it in the divorce even if she wanted it. If Gregorio burned it down on purpose, the only reason that makes sense is insurance fraud."

"What if he's committed a crime and needs the money to skip the country with his mistress?"

"Now you're projecting," I said.

"Kyle never cheated on me."

"That you know of." I watched her for a moment before changing the subject. "Let's look at this from a different angle. What if the wife hired someone to burn the house down? She picked a fight in public and then stayed there drinking afterward to establish her alibi. Maybe she's the spiteful one, huh?"

"Mm. Look, Ma, I have to get back to work. We can talk about this more tonight, okay?"

"Sure, honey."

"Okay, bye."

"Hey!"

"Yeah?"

"See what you can find out about the Ortizes, will you? I'd love to know what the police know."

"Mom! I can't do that! It wouldn't be right. It's my first day on the job."

"Technically, it's your second. Besides, you're not a cop. You didn't take a vow, did you?"

"No."

"So, help your mother out."

"Mom!"

"Diana! I need to find little Andy."

Diana sighed but gave in, as I knew she would. "I'll see what I can do," she said. "No promises."

"Thanks, honey."

♦♦♦

◆

Normals see Magick.
They just don't believe it.
They don't appreciate it.
They ignore it.
Reject it.
They call it Nature.
Coincidence.
Ridiculous.

—Op-Editorial from the Wyrdwood North Gazette

◆

15

MUSE
Proves that digging isn't just for dogs.

I had soil stuck to my paws—soil that was sticky with worm poop, dead bugs, and rotting leaves. To make matters worse, the Ortizes' lawn was covered with a layer of ash from the fire. It got trapped between my toes and tasted bitter, not unlike the funeral pyres of the Romans. Of course, the Romans ruined whatever they touched, not unlike the Ortizes did.

From the beginning of history, cats have walked alongside gods, humans, and kith ancestors. We've been adored by the highest royalty, and we've protected the most celebrated children from scorpions and spiders. We've prowled the darkest alleys in search of vermin.

In exchange, all we ask is a little veneration. Let me just say it plainly. We—meaning "I"—were meant to be worshipped. In ancient Egypt, cats were treated like gods. The Romans changed that. Stupid Romans.

Despite that betrayal, we cats have not forgotten our duties. To those who have called us lazy and said we have no care for anyone but ourselves, I would reply, "Try living without a cat for a month and see how overrun with mice and bugs your nest gets. That is our worth. Do not take us for granted."

Sadly, no one listens to me.

On that day in particular, I was on a mission. The yard outside the Ortiz house had hidden treasure, and I intended to find it.

I put my nose to good use, and when I caught an odd

smell, I scratched at the dirt until its source appeared. The first item I found was a tiny metal car lost by a tiny stupid boy. Annoyed, I moved on.

The second one I found was a plastic bag that contained a leather collar made for someone with a thick neck—probably humanoid. Despite the dirt, it sparkled with diamonds. I pulled it out with my paw. Whoever had buried it hadn't dug deep. It came out easily. I picked it up with my mouth and carried it to Greta's house, where I hid it in the crawlspace.

Next, I found a small fabric bag. I didn't know what it contained, but I added it to my pile.

I continued my search with smug satisfaction that whoever had buried their treasures would return to find them gone. It was a game I liked to play with squirrels too. Don't judge me. Someone's got to make their tiny lives interesting.

◆◆◆

◆

Done pretending to be Normal.

—T-shirt

◆

16

DIANA
Dives into the investigation.

The sheriff's office buzzed with electricity, not just from the old fluorescent fixtures, but also from the frenzied search for Anthony Ortiz. The presence of the kids' parents in the conference room with the glass walls made the deputies work harder to look busy. Every face had frustration and concentration on it.

The Ortizes had been there all day, yelling at people, sobbing on the conference table, and generally being annoying. Okay, it's possible "annoying" isn't the right word—or even a nice one. But, with the amount of time the deputies spent tending to *their* needs, they could have searched half the county for the missing kid.

Chief Deputy Nick Harding—I'd discovered his last name—recognized the problem and appeared beside my desk. "Look," he said, giving me what I was learning was his serious face. "I need a favor." I suspected it was never good when he said that.

"Okay," I replied, closing one eye.

He crouched down, putting himself below my eye level. I was seated. "I need you to handle the Ortizes. Get them drinks, food, whatever they need. Give them regular updates."

I raised my eyebrows.

"Thing is," he continued. "They're randomizing my deputies, and I can't have them interrupting every five minutes for another box of tissues."

I looked around the room. "So, you're asking the only

woman here to do it?"

Nick blinked. "You're not my only woman employee."

"No. But I'm the only one here. Vanessa is out sick. Auntie Kalea is visiting her mother in Hawaii, and Tetty is out on patrol. Why not ask Dane or Kemp? I have work..." I indicated my desk.

"I know it's a huge favor and not in your job description."

"I just don't want to set a precedent. I'm not your coffee-delivery girl. That's not me."

"I get it. Please, just this once. You'd be doing me a personal favor. So, will you do it?"

"Sure. As long as we're clear."

"We are." Nick stood again. "They're bringing Sheherezad Abbasi in now. I'm expecting drama from the Ortizes. They're serious about filing a lawsuit against the girl. We need to keep them separate."

"I'll find something to occupy them."

"Thanks, Diana. I mean it. I owe you one." Nick patted me on the shoulder as he walked away. I had a brief naughty thought about a way he could pay me back and then a scolding chat with myself. He's Boss, not Sexy Man. And I'm Bad Girl.

Later that morning, I took my lunch break. The peanut butter and jelly sandwich Mom had packed for me was surprisingly tasty. It beat eating the stale granola bar I've been saving for an emergency at the bottom of my backpack. Eating out wasn't in the budget—yet.

I sat at one of the tiny tables in the break room and watched the Ortizes. They were arguing again. Still. The only time they weren't arguing was when they were sulking in silence.

Both of them had lost their shine. The usual rich gleam of their eyes and teeth, of their jewels and sequins, had dimmed. They looked like regular people, tired and upset regular people.

"Hey," said Nick, sticking his head in the doorway and looking directly at me. Everyone else in the room turned to face him as well.

"Hey," I replied, licking peanut butter off the roof of my mouth.

"Did you order lunch for the Ortizes?"

"No."

"Find out what they want and have it delivered. Jerry at the front desk will pay for it."

"You mean the tax payers will pay for it." I took another bite of my sandwich.

Nick hung on the doorframe a moment longer, watching me, before leaving back the way he'd come.

"You're welcome!" I called after him, not too loudly.

"Thank you!" he called back from out of sight.

The others in the break-room stared at me.

"What?" I asked.

They jumped back to their own business.

For a small town, Wyrdwood had a surprising number of restaurants, diners, and cafés. In the interest of avoiding another fight, I picked the Thai-Chinese-American fusion place—Our Pad—and presented it to the Ortizes as the only option.

They didn't object. Badahlia wasn't hungry, but Gregorio, with surprising thoughtfulness, told me to order vegetable Pad See Ew for her so she'd have it if she changed her mind. I called in what they wanted and added an extra sweet and sour chicken—for me. The sandwich hadn't sated me, and I was stuck at the office taking care of them. I figured that if I passed out from starvation, I would be of no use to the Ortizes. I was within protocol.

While we were waiting, my phone rang. When I saw who

it was, I cringed and almost didn't answer. It rang again, and like Pavlov's dog I automatically hit the button. With the phone to my ear, I headed for the computer room seeking privacy. I had time. The display said it was the prison—Snake River Correctional Institution. It was an appropriate name for a place where they incarcerated snakes. To add insult to injury, the county where it resided was Malheur County. "Malheur"—in case you don't know—is French for "unhappiness" or "bad luck." Which came first? Chicken? Egg? Prison? Name?

A recorded voice spoke to me, "This is the Snake River Correctional Institution. You have a collect call from…"

The voice changed to one I recognized. "Kyle Butts."

"Will you accept the charges?"

I sighed. "Do I have to?" I wondered aloud, shutting myself in the computer room.

The recording said, "Press or say 'one' for yes or 'two' for no."

I closed my eyes and leaned back against the door. Resigned, I said, "One."

It always took a while for the connection to happen. I debated my decision to take the call. Kyle *was* my husband. And he was a felon. I'd loved him. And he'd destroyed my world. He claimed to still love me. But he never called unless he wanted something.

That same old black cloud hovered over my head and began to suck all the oxygen from the room.

"Hey, Babe," he said. "Thanks for taking my call."

My eyes steamed up, and I couldn't speak. His beautiful, familiar, seductive voice got to me every time.

After letting the silence sit for a minute, he said, "How are you? You doing okay?"

That broke me from the spell.

I said, "No."

"What's the matter? Talk to me. I love you, Babe."

"Forget it. What do you want?"

"No, nothing. I just wanted to hear your voice and see how you're doing. I worry about you, you know?"

So many recriminations rose from my throat and sat right behind my teeth.

A little too little, a little too late.

Why now? You weren't worried about me when you risked going to prison.

Hah! Liar!

But, Kyle and I had gone around and around all that, more times than I could count. I'd eventually decided it hurt my heart too much to punish him for what he'd done, and it was pointless. Our marriage had changed—irreparably.

"Okay," I said. And left it at that.

"I do, Babe. I have lots of time to think in here, and I know how much I hurt you. I'm really sorry." He sounded sincere, but I'd heard it all before.

"Okay," I said.

"Don't you love me anymore?"

I didn't know the answer. I missed him in bed. I missed his smell, his warmth, and the sound of his breathing. I missed waking up beside him. Memories of the happy times haunted me. Sometimes I heard his laughter, and once I thought I spotted him on the street. He had become my own personal ghost. I was his widow.

A part of me wished he were dead. It would be so much easier to grieve and move on.

On the darkest nights, I kicked myself. I thought I could have prevented all this if I'd paid close enough attention to what he was doing. If I'd nagged him more. If I'd made him want to be home so badly that he didn't have time to build a criminal empire. If only I'd—

"Babe, listen. Wouldn't it be great if you came to see me? I know I've avoided it, because I've been ashamed, but I'm ready. I miss your smile."

Once upon a time, that kind of emotional plea would have struck home. I, however, remembered the past six months since his arrest very differently. He made it sound like he was the one who'd not wanted a visit. The truth was that I always found an excuse not to go. Every time.

Oh, ye king of gaslighting. You don't even realize you've lost me.

"No," I said.

"No what?"

"No, I don't love you anymore."

A small squeak sounded from the far corner of the computer room.

I narrowed my eyes in that direction.

"Babe, c'mon," Kyle whined. "When are you going to forgive me? I'm doing my time."

I walked toward the squeak.

"It's so lonely in here. And the other guys are dangerous. They threaten my life every day. I just need you to understand."

I stopped to focus on the phone. At last, he was getting to the point. "Whatever you want, Kyle, forget about it."

"You're my wife—for better or for worse, remember?"

A quiet shuffling came from the back of the room. Someone or some thing was definitely there. I followed the sound.

"You broke that vow. Not me." I peeked around the edge of a shelf unit to discover two pairs of wide, terrified eyes looking up at me.

"I didn't mean to. I did it all for you, so you'd have the kind of life you deserved."

My fury must have shown on my face because Deputy Ben and Josie the temp shuffled out from behind the shelves. Ben kept himself between me and her while she finished buttoning her blouse back up. They scuttled past me and out the door. I watched them go. My anger at Kyle turned bitter because I once had what Ben and Josie did—

and he'd ruined it.

I realized Kyle was still speaking, trying a rambling series of apologies and self-recriminating statements he didn't truly mean. I no longer believed a word he said.

Not true. I believed him when he said, "I need you to send me some money, Babe."

I laughed. I couldn't help it. It struck me funny, and once I'd started, I couldn't stop. I sounded hysterical, even to myself. Laugh-tears streamed down my face.

"Babe?"

"I have to go," I said between chuckles.

"No, wait. Babe, I—"

I hung up on him. It felt great. No, it felt monumental. So why did my laugh-tears suddenly turn into real tears? I slid into Ben and Josie's hiding place and cried for the loss of my marriage.

My phone buzzed and interrupted my self-indulgence. Jerry at the front desk had texted to let me know lunch had arrived. I dried my tears and put my work face on.

The Ortizes were alone when I carried the food in to them, but their lawyer arrived while I was setting it out.

One of three partners at the Bagley, Smart, and Cobb law offices, Divana Smart wore a 1940s-style pantsuit in antique white. No one would've been surprised if she'd arrived on a white horse. The world around her paled in comparison. It was difficult not to stare.

She stopped on the threshold to the room. "Good afternoon, Mr. Ortiz. Mrs. Ortiz," she said, her voice a river of chocolate. "Mind if I come in?"

Both parents turned toward her. "Please," said Gregorio. "Join us. Have a seat."

Ms. Smart inclined her head and glided to a chair at the table. She set her briefcase upon it, sat down, folded her hands with their long, graceful fingers, then looked pointedly at me. She caught me watching her.

I quickly shifted my gaze away and made myself busy with the food. I could sense her eyes on me.

"Don't worry about her," Gregorio said. "She's a secretary here. So, what did you find out? Can we sue her?"

I glared at the napkins I was laying out on the table so I wouldn't glare directly at him. Secretary? Secretary!

Ms. Smart opened her briefcase before answering, "Yes, and no. There is no question that the young lady in question was negligent in her duties. However, she is only seventeen and has no assets to speak of. What exactly is the goal of suing her?"

Badahlia spoke up quickly. "We want her to pay."

"You want to punish her?" Ms. Smart revealed no judgment in her question. She merely wanted clarification.

Gregorio replied, "Yes. We trusted her with our son."

With growing emotion, Badahlia said, "She hasn't even apologized. She has no idea what she's done or that she's responsible for it. She may even be working with whoever has him. The police say she doesn't know anything. They refuse to arrest her." Badahlia's voice rose to a fever pitch. "She's the only one who was there! She was supposed to be keeping him safe!"

I found myself frozen, holding a white carton of pad see yew in my hands.

Ms. Smart lowered the temperature in the room with her tone. "Until we know what happened to Anthony, there is no crime. We have a missing boy. If it turns out that Sheherezad Abbasi's negligence was a factor, then I'm sure the mayor will take the appropriate action. I spoke with her this morning, and she will be putting her own investigator on your boy's trail. They'll find him."

"But this is Wyrdwood," whined Badahlia. "There are perverts and cannibals on every block! Gods only know what they're doing to him."

With a cool-headed gesture, Ms. Smart replied, "And every one of those perverts and cannibals knows the laws here. They abide by them, or they suffer the consequences."

By then, I had removed all the items from the delivery bags, and I had no more excuse to stay. I said a polite, "Excuse me," and left the room.

My desk had a direct line of sight to the conference room, so I sat there, nibbling at my vegetable fried rice and observing the rest of their conversation. I wished I could read lips, though I didn't have to. Ms. Smart had a calming effect on Badahlia, and the rest of the meeting centered on the signing of papers.

The lawyer impressed me. When finally, she closed her briefcase and stood, I was ready. I leapt to my feet and hurried to meet her outside the conference room. I heard the last of her goodbyes as she emerged then fell into step with her on the way to the stairs.

I tried to find my words and failed. If my insecurities had had their way, I'd have walked all the way to her car with her without saying a word.

Fortunately, Divana Smart had keen intuition. She stopped, turned to face me, and offered her hand. A gentle smile greeted me. "I'm Divana Smart of Bagley, Smart, and Cobb."

I hesitated then shook her hand. "Hi."

"And you are?" she asked.

"Oh, sorry. I'm Diana Kats. I'm...I'm a network specialist here. I work for these guys." I indicated the surrounding building.

"I see. And, how can I help you, Ms. Kats?"

I spit the words out as quickly as I could, "I need to get a divorce." My bottom lip trembled of its own accord.

"I can help." No three words had ever felt so kind.

Divana Smart's gaze never faltered. "Come see me in my office on Monday, after you get off work. 6 p.m. Bring your marriage certificate, if you have it."

I nodded, at a loss for words. I didn't want to be emotional. I didn't want the huge lump in my throat. I was doing the right thing. Why did letting go have to be so painful?

After a brief wait for me to reply, Ms. Smart rested her hand on my shoulder and stepped past me. "I'll see you Monday, Ms. Kats."

I watched her glide down the stairs and was still standing there when the Ortizes pushed past me, one on either side. They said nothing to me.

◆◆◆

◆

**Men are like cats.
If you're allergic to them,
You're a challenge.**

—Old wives' tale

◆

17

KITTY
Bribes Val with pie.

After the spa, I stopped at the grocery store to get bread, milk, and cat food. While I was there, I found a beautiful cherry pie. Cherries were in season. On instinct, I bought two. You can never have too many pies.

I was almost home when I spotted the Ortizes on Valentine Krall's front lawn. Valentine Krall was sixty if he was a day, and he had mastered the grouchy old man schtick. His neck slumped forward, as if he spent all his time looking down, and his face and body were all angles and sharp corners. What remained of his dark hair was hanging on by a wish and a prayer.

Badahlia and Val shouted at each other, waved their arms, and stomped their feet. If I didn't know better, I'd have said it was an Italian flirtation. Gregorio stood to one side, wisely making no move to get involved.

Badahlia shouted, "This is all your fault, Krall!"

With equal vehemence, Val shouted back, "It is not *my* fault you can't control your offspring!"

I gave a brief thought to the milk in my grocery bag then pulled to the curb. Someone needed to calm them down before they came to blows.

"You did something to him, didn't you!"

"What do you think I did?"

"I don't know. But you hated him!"

"I hate all kids, lady! Yours included."

"Ever since you accused him of stealing your wood,

you've had it in for him!"

I got out of the car and approached on an angle.

"He stole it. I showed you the video of him sneaking into my workshop."

"That proves nothing!"

"I suppose you think I hired a kid crisis actor that looks like him?"

"Don't be an asshole. You know what I'm saying. He didn't intend to steal. He was just curious. God! You're a jerk!"

Val's eyes hardened, and he started, "And you're a—"

"Excuse me!" I interrupted him, somewhat sharply.

Val looked at me then back at Badahlia. His voice softened but not in kindness. "It shows him leaving with the wood, sneaking away like the thief he is. I'm going to guess you didn't discipline him? Did you find my wood?"

"He said you gave him that wood, and I believe my son. It's just like you to frame him for a crime he didn't commit. Are you punishing him? Is that it? Is he in your house?" Badahlia made a move as if to enter Val's residence.

My eyes widened. No one had ever been inside Val's. He was a neurotically private person—which, admittedly, was suspicious in and of itself.

Val stepped in front of her, blocking her way. "He's not in there," he said low and threatening.

They stared at each other, furious.

"Excuse me?" I repeated. "Can we just take a breath, please? Badahlia, I'm sure Val had no hand in your son's disappearance."

"He knows something," Badahlia said.

Val shook his head. "I don't know anything about it. Now, get out of my yard before I call the sheriff."

Gregorio finally saw his opening and stepped forward to take hold of his wife's arm. "Badahlia, let's go. This is pointless."

Badahlia jerked her arm out of his grasp and pointed at Val. "If I find out you had *anything* to do with Ant'ony's disappearance, I'll kill you. Do you hear me? I'll kill you."

"You realize," said Val, deadpan, "that you just said that in front of witnesses?"

With a wave of her arm to dismiss him, Badahlia turned to go. Under her breath, she said, "I'll kill them all."

Wide-eyed, I watched her go. Eventually, only Val and I remained on the lawn.

"Dang," I said.

Val nodded. "And people wonder why the kid would run away."

"You deserve a pie after that." I trotted to my car and pulled out one of the pies I'd just bought. I headed straight for his front door. This strategic move, I might add, was not my own idea. I'd seen it on TV.

"Hey!" Val called, tearing his attention away from Gregorio and Badahlia.

"I'll just set it on your counter. It's safer that way." I didn't wait for an answer but barged inside.

Val followed me in on my heels.

"Where's your kitchen?" I asked.

The interior of Val's house was very different from the exterior. While well-kept, the outside had the simplicity of a middle-class ranch-style home. Val mowed his own lawn and had a few peony bushes along the front wall, and that was it. His front door had no window. As a matter of fact the only windows were short and wide, high on the wall. He obviously didn't care to look out at his neighbors—nor to have them look in.

The interior, on the other hand, deserved a spread in 'Homes of the Rich and Famous.' I stepped into an open-concept living room/kitchen in a Southwest style. Wood flooring complemented the earthy stucco walls. A giant fireplace occupied one wall, and a giant flatscreen TV took up most of the other.

Skylights in the ceiling cast a surprising amount of light down upon the room, highlighting paintings of desert vistas with their blue skies, saguaro cacti, and blooming paloverde trees. His furniture was modern. It exuded comfort and masculine roughness simultaneously. His kitchen had an island and the kind of appliances I'd kill for, and a dog bed in the corner held the sleeping form of Val's elderly pug, famously named Winston.

I immediately pegged Val as a Taurus.

"What a lovely space," I said as I crossed toward the kitchen. "You have an eye for decor."

"I'm an architect." Val couldn't hide that he was flattered, but it didn't last. "You don't have to give me a pie."

"Oh, but I do." I took my time. The decor had a masculine aesthetic, but Val liked to be comfortable. He had tossed a velour throw on the couch and thick rugs hugged the floor. A Mexican china cabinet held statuary and family photos, including one of Val with a teenage boy—a chip off the ol' block, as they say.

I said, "The Ortizes are in a terrible position right now, with their son missing. They don't mean to be rude."

"Right," said Val, obviously disbelieving. "This wasn't my first rodeo with the Ortizes. I know exactly how they are. They think that boy shits gold nuggets. It wouldn't surprise me if the kid burned the place down on purpose."

"What? That's a horrible thought. I hope not!"

Val shrugged. "Like a good neighbor, I informed them that the boy had broken into my garage and stolen some balsa I use to make models. They wouldn't even consider the possibility that he had. That woman called me a liar, to my face."

I blinked in surprise. "You said you had video of it?"

"I've got cameras all around my property."

"Oh. And you showed them the footage?"

"Of course. Didn't matter. They made up some story in their heads about how I'd set him up. I let it go. After the way they treated me, it wasn't worth the effort. I didn't care about the wood. It only cost me fifteen dollars. Only reason I went over at all was 'cause I figured they'd want to correct their son's behavior."

"Sure. *Most* parents would want to know if their kid was turning into a delinquent."

"Exactly what I thought. But not the Ortizes. Like son, like father, eh?"

"What do you mean?"

"Gregorio's been inching the boundary of his property onto the Garrett's for years. An inch at a time. This year, he planted those bushes beyond the line, on the Garrett side. They're a family of thieves, and the Garretts are too oblivious to notice."

"How do you know where their property line is?"

"I remember when they put in that concrete driveway and had a surveyor from the city mark the edge. I'll never forget Gregorio's senile old father standing on the lawn in his skivvies shouting at the workers."

I snorted a laugh. I couldn't help it. "Wow. Sorry you had to see that."

A small smile touched the corner of Val's mouth. He nodded slowly. "I've seen a lot in this neighborhood. Like how Ortiz the Younger was at the house before the fire department arrived. Got that on camera too."

"Yeah, we know he was there with a babysitter."

"No, not the kid. Emmanuel."

"Manny?"

"Yeah. The one who got shysted out of his inheritance."

"What do you mean?"

Val studied me for a minute, then asked, "Do you actually live in this neighborhood?"

"I do," I insisted, "but apparently I've had my head—"

"Up your butt?"

I blinked. "I was going to say 'in a hole,' but yeah. So... go on."

"Well, Manny got diddly-squat. Pissed his father off when he refused to go into the family business."

"No kidding!"

"Yeah. You know they're all corporate lawyers, right? Well, everyone except Emmanuel—Manny. He's a cook."

Manny wasn't a cook. He was a cookbook author—a rather successful one from what I could gather. What I didn't know was that he'd been cut out of his father's will. And who knew Val was such a busy-body? I was thanking my lucky stars I'd bought two pies.

"So you saw Manny at the house the night of the fire?"

"Skulking around in the dark. I've seen him do it before too, but I always figured it was some kind of jealous stalking. You know, because of the inheritance."

I couldn't believe my ears. "What was he doing?"

"No idea."

"Can I see the footage?"

"Sure. Give me your email address, and I'll send you a copy." Val crossed to a tiny desk in the kitchen and produced a notepad and pen. I set the pie on the counter and wrote down my email.

"Thanks, Val." I handed him the pad and realized he'd tricked me into giving up my excuse for being there. He'd placed himself between me and the pie.

"Thanks for the pie, Kitty. I'll see you later." He gestured toward the door.

I left meekly, aware that I'd been outmaneuvered. On the way out, I passed a bookshelf. I paused to examine the books. Most were on the subject of architecture, but there was also a shelf full of romantic suspense novels written by Anise Hyssop.

"Ooh," I said, pointing at the books. "My daughter loves

this author. She buys the new ones as soon as they come out."

Val opened the front door and stood there, hinting that I should leave. I couldn't think of a way to stay longer without looking like I was nosing around—which I was—so I joined him on the threshold. Before crossing it, I asked, "Say, I don't suppose you have cameras trained on *my* house, do you?"

"Not since Bob died," he said. "Wouldn't be right."

I wasn't sure what that meant, but Val was pushing me out the door and closing it on me.

"Bye, Kitty," he said. "Thanks for the pie."

To his credit, he did send me a copy of the security video. I watched it on my phone in the car, then called Diana—milk forsaken.

◆◆◆

◆

Fail fast, fail spectacularly.

—Diana's motto

◆

18

DIANA
Runs into an old rival.

I was loving my new job and feeling powerful after my encounter with Divana Smart—but then Brenda Doill came by my desk. Brenda was an old rival from junior high. She'd been a bully then, and I'd been her target. To say that she'd been one of the pretty girls was not quite accurate. She'd been okay and had made up the extra popularity points with her extroversion. She dated all the most-wanted boys and won all the competitions. When she was around, she was leading the shenanigans. She was never boring, to say the least.

I hadn't seen her in years, so when she suddenly appeared beside me, my childhood trauma gave me an adrenaline rush similar to what a mouse gets when a cat appears. Fight or flight? Well, I froze.

"So it *is* you," Brenda said. "I didn't believe it when they told me."

"Brenda," I replied with the last of my breath.

"Diana Banana." It was not a term of endearment. She'd started calling me that in middle school after sexualizing how I ate a banana in the cafeteria—in front of everyone.

I remembered to suck in air.

She said, "It takes a lot of nerve coming back here to Wyrdwood, after...everything. How is ol' Dirty Butts, anyway?" Her voice took on a tone of fake concern. "Is he doing okay in prison?"

"No idea."

"Well, I see *you* managed to stay out of prison."

"I had nothing to do with it."

"Uh huh." She nodded her head over her shoulder to indicate the boss's office. "I'm just here to see Nick. He and I are dating. He know about the skeleton in your closet?"

My mouth soured, and I swallowed.

Brenda smiled.

Before I could think of a good come-back, my phone rang. A glance at the screen told me it was Mom.

"I have to take this," I said, getting up from my desk. "Excuse me."

"Say hi to Butts for me," she chirped to my back.

I kept walking.

"Mom," I said into the phone, "hold on while I find some privacy." I entered a small glass-walled meeting room and shut the door. I held the phone to my ear and watched Brenda knock at Nick's office. She glanced back at me then slithered inside.

I said, "Okay. What's up?"

Mom was beyond pleasantries. She dove right in. "What have you found out about the Ortizes?"

"I've been working, Mom. I don't have time to snoop for you." Actually, I didn't want to talk about it at work. The walls had ears.

"Well, while you've been *working,* I've been investigating." She made it sound like I'd been goofing off. "Did you know that Papa Ortiz cut Manny out of his will because Manny didn't go into law?" She didn't wait for a reply. "It's true. And there's more. I already have five possible suspects!"

My boss, the attractive man known as Nick, walked by outside the room. Brenda was nowhere in sight.

Nick saw me and gave me a nod and a smile, both of which I returned. My body experienced an unexpected thrill. I turned my back on him.

"That's great, Ma. Can we talk about it when I get home?"

"I guess. But I'm catsitting tonight at the Garrett's place. Come by there. I'll make dinner. What time do you get off work?"

I knew better than to fall for that trap. If I told her a time, she'd expect me then, and if I was late, I'd be in trouble. "I'm not sure. I'm troubleshooting a nasty software bug, and there's no way to predict how long that'll take. I'll call you when I'm on my way, okay?" I wasn't exactly lying. There was a bug, but it would probably take me several days to track down—unless I got lucky.

"All right, honey. Just see if you can't find a minute or two to see where the Ortiz case is, please. Find out if they have any leads."

"I'll do what I can, Mom. No promises." I was the queen of noncommittal communication when it came to my mother. Safer that way.

"Oh, and don't cook. I have leftover pad see ew from lunch today." Actually, the Ortizes hadn't touched a bite of what I'd ordered for them.

"You didn't eat the sandwich I made for you?"

"Gotta go, Ma. I'll talk to you later."

"I'm making curry! You can eat the pad for lunch tomorrow."

"Okay," I said. "I gotta go." I was already hanging up.

Shortly thereafter, Nick stopped by my desk.

I held my breath, waiting for the magic words, "Come see me in my office." Or, "Clean out your desk." Brenda Doill wouldn't have missed another opportunity to make my life miserable. Some things never change. Some people.

Instead, he said, "Take a look at this." He held out a photograph. "What do you see?"

I took it. In the photo, Gregorio Ortiz was walking in the front door of an apartment complex. "It's Mr. Ortiz."

"Yeah. What else?"

"It's...night-time?"

"What else?"

I studied the photo but didn't see what he obviously wanted me to see—until I saw it. And then, I couldn't unsee it. Just beyond Gregorio, standing in a clump of bushes, hidden in shadow, pretending to be a trick of the light, was a large person. Its outline was indistinct until I focused my attention on it. I felt the zing in my bloodstream, and a face emerged. Definitely humanoid, the entity was watching Gregorio. No doubt in my mind.

"There's someone else there," I said.

"Exactly."

"Someone sneaking around, watching him. You think it's the kidnapper?"

"I don't know. You think you can enhance it?"

That wasn't exactly my area of expertise, but to the Luddites among us, anyone who can do a little with computers must be able to do it all.

"It'll be tough enhancing their real face," I said, trying to squint and see it better. The being's features were somehow distorted to take advantage of the shadows. It could have been someone using magick or just face paint. It was tough to tell in a photo. Devices like cameras and video recorders rarely captured the magickal being behind the disguise.

People with magickal blood were on a spectrum. At one end, the beings were all magickal, and on the other, the beings were all non-magickal—what we call Normal, capital N.

I was mostly human with some magickal blood, so I didn't have a magickal appearance that I needed to hide. Everyone just saw me. The being in the photo was too obfuscated to tell, but they were odd. I wasn't shocked by that. What shocked me was that the watcher was so obviously zeroed in on Gregorio and, if I wasn't mistaken, they had a digital camera in one hand—the rectangular kind people take on vacation with them.

"I'll give it my best shot," I told Nick.

When he turned to go, I said, "So, you're not going to fire me?"

He paused, threw a dark look over his shoulder at me, then replied, "Not today," and walked away.

◆

**In ancient times, cats were
worshipped as gods;
they have not forgotten this.**

—Terry Pratchett

◆

19

MUSE
Stalks a stalker.

Humans aren't like cats. When cats skulk, we look cool. When humans skulk, it looks suspicious. Manny the Man was the King of Suspicious Skulking. I'd been watching him. He kept walking around the burned house and kicking the rubble.

The firefighters had finally left. The Ortizes had too. All that remained was Manny.

I followed him at a safe distance, observing his behavior. He seemed to be looking for a place to poop, though that was unlikely. Several times, he crouched down and dug at the dirt with his fingers. Where once there had been luxurious grass, the fire had turned the ground into a sorrowful expanse of mud. What the fire folk hadn't trampled, the water had drowned.

Manny had carefully placed golf tees as markers for where he'd buried his treasures. They weren't there anymore. *I'd* carried them off. I'd piled them under the Garretts' stinkiest shrub. They reminded me of bones. I liked that.

◆◆◆

♦

**The path of Self-Doubt
is a dead-end street.**

—graffiti at the end of Danger Alley in Wyrdwood

♦

20

KITTY
Woos Greta.

I had too many thoughts in my head, so I turned them all off. I took my groceries to the Garretts' place, put the milk in the fridge, chopped some veggies and chicken, and filled the crock-pot with curry fixings. The leftovers from that would save me from having to cook for the rest of my stay. And, I had a pie.

Greta was hiding, which was a good sign. She didn't rush out to menace me, and that meant she'd at least begrudgingly accepted me. Either that, or she was napping.

I washed her dishes and put down fresh food and water for her. After scooping her box, I felt ready to address the chaos in my mind.

I sat down at the dining room table with a notepad and a pen. At the very top, I wrote "Who Started the Fire?"

I then drew out a grid with four columns. At the top of Column A, I put the word "Suspects." Above Column B, I wrote "Alibi." C: "Motive." And D: "Notes."

Under "Suspects," I filled in Gregorio Ortiz, Badahlia Ortiz, Val Krall, Manny Ortiz, and Mistress (I.D. unknown).

I marked Gregorio, Manny, and Val as having no alibi. Badahlia had an alibi until shortly before midnight, so I just crossed her off.

Each one of them had a motive that I could see, although none of the motives seemed strong enough to risk the life of a young boy. It occurred to me that the fire might have been an accident, the result of nabbing Anthony. Say, he fought.

A candle got knocked over. I imagined the scene, and it brought tears to my eyes. Then, it occurred to me that he wouldn't have fought anyone in his family. Only a stranger. I wiped my eyes and made a note of it.

The doorbell rang.

Eli stood on the porch, holding a bouquet of tulips.

When I'd peered out through the curtains, he saw me, so I was forced to open the door. "Hi, Eli. What can I do for you?"

"I stopped by to see if there were any smoldering embers left. I brought tulips."

I looked down at my fingertips, trying to decide whether he'd used a double-entendre on purpose or not.

When I didn't immediately reply, he slid past me and headed for the kitchen. "I'll just put these on the counter for you. Do you have a vase?"

Shocked and outwitted for the second time that day, I closed the door and followed him. "I don't live here," I said.

"I know. Surely the people who live here have vases." With the flowers in one hand, he started opening cabinets.

I hurried forward to the right one. "Here! I saw one in here." I pulled down a cheap florist's vase. To get to the sink, I had to brush past Eli. I felt the sturdiness of his body then had to remind myself where I was going.

Eli came to stand beside me. "So…" He watched the water fill the vase. "Are you and Valentine a thing now?"

"What?"

"I saw you take a pie into his house. He's a good guy—though a little too old for you, don't you think?"

I stared up at him. "Val and me? No. He's a neighbor, that's all."

"Mm," said Eli, sounding relieved. "If you ask me, you're too good for him."

The water in the vase overflowed on my hands. I rushed

to turn off the faucet. "He's just a neighbor."

"That guy has more cameras around his house than a porn studio."

"Excuse me?"

"Not that I would know about porn studios. It's just an expression."

I dumped out the excess water and moved the vase to the countertop, placing it between Eli and me. "Mm." Subconsciously, I mimicked his "Mm" and only realized it after it came out. I considered telling him about Val's video footage, but I didn't want to give up my biggest chance at the reward. Eli, being a fire official and a stickler for the rules, would probably insist I turn it in. Instead, I asked, "Any more news about the fire next door?"

Eli carefully pulled the tulips from their paper, his hands gentle. "I signed off officially on the determination. It was an accident. The lights went out. The boy lit a candle and dropped it or set it near a curtain. No malicious intent."

"What happened to the lights?"

"They went out shortly before the fire started. The babysitter says she thought the kid had turned them off. She was already out in her boyfriend's car."

"The babysitter," I said.

"Yeah." Eli slid the flower stems into the vase then arranged them to present their best faces forward.

"Do you believe Anthony did that?"

"No idea. The fusebox was badly damaged by the fire, but we could tell that the main switch was flipped off."

"You're sure."

"One hundred percent."

"Can that happen...spontaneously? The switch flipping?"

Eli waggled his head from side to side. "Never say never?"

"Where was the fusebox?"

"In the mudroom off the kitchen." Eli picked up the vase

and carried it to the dining table. "What smells so good in here? You cooking?"

"Chicken curry."

My chart caught his eye. "What's this?" He picked it up before I could snatch it away.

"Just a thought exercise," I said, trying to take it from him. He turned so it was just out of my reach. I tried to stretch around without touching him. It was impossible. He smelled like Irish soap. "Give it back," I ordered.

He did, an amused smile on his face. "Kitty Kats, Private Detective."

I wasn't sure if he was mocking me or not, so I just turned my back on him and walked to the other side of the kitchen.

"Sorry to ruin your puzzle for you. The fire wasn't intentional."

"No," I said. "But the blackout might've been. And that's more than a little suspicious, considering there's a boy still missing."

"Ahhhh." Eli dismissed the idea with a wave of his hand. "Boys will be boys. That kid's probably hiding somewhere, eating dog food, because he's afraid he's in trouble for setting the house on fire. I'll bet you ten bucks he shows up tomorrow or the next day when he gets hungry enough."

I wasn't so ready to give up on the boy. "Thanks for the flowers," I said. "I'm sure you have a busy evening planned, and Diana will be here soon, so I need to get ready."

Jokingly—but not—he said, "You sure you don't need help with that chicken curry?"

"No, thanks. It was good to see you, Eli." I headed for the front door, opened it, and waited for him to go out.

He did, albeit reluctantly. "I'll see you soon, Kitty." He bent to hug me or kiss me or *something* me, and I stepped back out of reach.

"See you soon. You take care now." I closed the door on him, just as Val had done to me. Through the window, I watched Eli go to his truck and get in. I felt a little guilty for being so cold with him, but I couldn't encourage that kind of behavior. Not even a little.

I wasn't the kind of widow who would leap into the arms of the first man who paid attention to her. I could stand on my own two feet, and I'd prove it.

But, dang, he'd smelled good.

I shut the door, and when I turned around, Greta was there, on all fours, hunkered down as if preparing to pounce. She hissed at me.

"Oh sure," I said. "You come out *after* the big man is gone. I guess he woke you up from your nap, huh?"

I looked around for an object to place between me and her. I didn't want a cat fight. The coat rack beside the door had a raincoat on it.

"Now, Greta," I said, keeping my voice low and calm. "Don't be like that. I'm your friend. I'm here take care of you. The man is gone."

Greta growled a warning.

Moving very slowly, I took the coat off the rack and held it like a bull-fighter.

Greta made a little lunging movement, menacing me, but she didn't attack. It struck me as adorable. This tiny creature, so fluffy and normally sweet-faced, had become a warrior and was standing up to what she perceived as a gi-ant invader in her home—me.

"It's okay, honey," I said. "You're okay. I'm not going to eat you." I averted my eyes while keeping her in my periph-eral vision. The eyes are everything with cats. Staring at a cat is sure to get you in trouble unless they want you to stare. "I'm here to help you. Your mom asked me to take care of you. Are you hungry?"

Greta was staring at me, wide-eyed and unblinking.

"You're a good girl," I told her and inched toward the kitchen, keeping the hem of the raincoat between us like a toreador. "You're safe."

Greta lunged again. Her threatening gesture made me jump. It was a primal reaction—ancestral memories of being stalked by a lion, perhaps.

"No," I said in my mom-voice. "No, no, no." Most kitties understood that word. I tried the slow blink again.

Sometimes, you just had to wait them out. Emotions were hard for kitties, especially anger, fear, and sadness. They often lashed out for those reasons. So, I waited for her to calm down.

And waited.

And waited.

Eyes averted. I waited some more. She was stubborn!

Eventually, however, she backed up a few steps. Just backed away. She wasn't about to turn her back on me.

"Good girl," I said gently and rewarded her with another slow blink.

Moving one paw at a time, she began to go, keeping one eye on me the whole way. This was the moment when the tide turned, and she gave up on getting me out. She was slinking away to fight another day. It meant we'd reached another level in our relationship.

"Good girl, Greta."

That was when a loud knock sounded on the door at my back. Loud enough to make me jump. Loud enough to make Greta slip and slide on hardwood in an attempt to run away as fast as possible.

So much for winning her trust.

I heaved a sigh and turned around to open the door. "Eli, I told you—"

A real giant loomed in the doorway. I nearly hissed at him.

"Kitty Kats?" the man said in a voice as deep as mountains.

"Yes?"

"I'm investigating the Ortiz kid's disappearance. They tell me you were here that night? I'd like to ask you some questions. Your neighbor Mike Cook said I should talk to you."

The sun was setting, and it was getting dark enough that he was cloaked in shadow. I switched on the porch light.

"Let me see your badge," I demanded. If I'd been twenty years younger and less suspicious, I'd have found him attractive. In his mid-thirties-ish, he wore casual clothes and what looked like a motorcycle jacket, though the vehicle parked at the curb was a nondescript sedan—the same nondescript sedan I'd seen the night before.

The man shook his head. "Not a cop. Private contractor. Eagle Crenshaw."

I thought about that and came to the conclusion that he was probably after the reward. He was my competition. I narrowed my eyes. "Okay. What do you want to know?" I was not letting him into Pamela's house, but I could try to draw information from him. After all, he didn't know that I was investigating it too.

"One of your neighbors reported seeing someone lurking around the Ortiz property on the night of the fire. An adult. Did you see anyone?"

A memory of the video flashed in my mind. "Did they describe this person?"

"Nobody got a good look. I was hoping you'd be able to give me more."

"I'm afraid not."

"Have you noticed anything suspicious since you've been staying here?"

"Like what?"

"Missing objects? Prowlers? Strange cars parked on the street."

I wanted to say, "Only yours," but I refrained. "Have things been going missing?" I asked.

"Nothing of significance. Some lawn furniture cushions. It could be completely unrelated, but I have to ask."

"Ah." I leaned against the doorframe, mimicking his pose. "I haven't noticed anything out of the ordinary. What are your instincts telling you about the boy? You think someone took him?"

Eagle fell for my mirroring tactics. His shoulders relaxed. "Right now, I'm leaning toward it being a family member. I can't say more than that."

"I guess that means you don't work for the family?"

He didn't answer, saying instead, "I'm considering the possibility that this is kith drama."

I studied him, wondering if I should discuss that with him. "What do you mean?"

"You've got the Sight, yes?"

With a deep breath, I looked him over. "I better, seeing as how you're breaking about ten laws right now if I don't."

"Yeah, sorry. Your neighbor said you descend from dakini ancestry."

"Oh, he volunteered that, did he?" I was shocked, frankly. The guy must have won Mike over. I imagined them bumping fists and drinking beers together.

"Your secret's safe with me."

"It better be," I replied and meant the threat. I planned to have a stern talk with Mike Cook at my earliest convenience. "Fair's fair," I said. "Tit for tat?"

"Huh?"

"What's your kin? You know mine. I should know yours."

"Oh! Right. I'm a Normal."

My eyes narrowed, and my jaw tightened.

He hurried to explain. "An awakened one, though. I grew up in a foster home with dragonkin. They let me in when I was eleven, though I have no spark."

"The mayor knows?"

"Of course. I registered. I'm allergic to execution."

That made me smile. "Understandable." Despite myself, I was starting to like this guy—my competition. I said, "So you think this might be some kind of kith feud or a predator or what?"

He shrugged. "Dunno. Just looking for anything I might be missing. I'm out of the loop when it comes to kith politics."

"Because of your handicap?" I couldn't help it. I half-smiled.

"Yeah. My normality." He smiled too, though more wryly.

"I haven't seen any particular sign of kith involvement. Did the neighbors sense something?"

He shook his head. "Nah."

"Look, I have dinner cooking. I need to go back inside. You have a good night." I shoved off the doorframe and said, rather disingenuously, "I hope you find the boy."

"I hope so too. Thanks for your time. You're catsitting here, right? But you live up the street?"

"That's right." It occurred to me that he may think my house was unattended and vulnerable for Heaven knew what. I didn't trust him. I said, "My daughter's staying in my house, though. She works for the sheriff."

"Your daughter?"

"Yeah. And her friend." The truth was that Diana had only one friend: Mini-Mimi. But this nosy Nellie didn't know that. "Good night." I went inside. I heard him wish me the same, just as I closed—and locked—the door.

I was still peering out through a crack in the curtains, watching him drive down the block, when Diana strode up the walk with Mimi on a leash. I opened the door and waved them inside.

"Sorry I'm so late," she said. "I had to feed and walk Mimi."

I peeked again, just to make sure Eagle Crenshaw wasn't

coming back.

"What are you doing?" she asked.

"Nothing." I gently guided Diana toward the kitchen. "You hungry? They're calling the fire next door an accident."

"Okay. That's a relief, right?"

"No." I pulled out a stool at the counter for her.

"No?"

I set the chart I'd made in front of her. "We need to create a timeline of that night."

Diana studied the chart, far more intrigued and far less condescending than Eli had been. "Sure, why not? But first, I have news."

"They found the Ortiz boy?"

"No."

"Phew!" I sighed with relief then realized how that sounded. "I mean 'oh no.'"

Diana rolled her eyes toward me without moving her head and continued, "The babysitter showed up at the station to speak to the sheriff. The Ortizes were there. They might be pressing charges against her."

"For what?"

"For leaving the boy alone in the house."

◆◆◆

♦

**It's better to be a snowflake
than a flake, a fake,
or a snake.**

— seen on a beer coaster

♦

21

KITTY
Enlists Diana's help to find clues.

Curry chicken heals all. I set a bowl of my special recipe in front of Diana.

"Your boss must trust you to put the Ortizes in your care. How did you keep them occupied?"

"Glad you asked, Mom," she replied. "I'd been going through all the apps that the station uses, and I found one with pictures of bad guys. Remember the old-fashioned mug-shot books you've seen on TV? Well, like that, but digital. I set them up in front of it and let them look for anyone they'd seen lurking around them lately. I'm kind of a genius, you know?"

"Oh, I know," I said. "You tell me often enough." I retrieved a bowl of curry for myself and sat down opposite her. "Was there drama when Sherry showed up? She still hasn't called me back, by the way."

"I imagine she's been kind of busy. Y'know?"

"You're right. But it's just manners."

"To answer your question, no, there was no drama. They snuck Sherry in the back way, so the Ortizes never even saw her. I watched the interview though."

"You did?"

"Yeah. I tapped into the video feed. Not sure how legal that is, but I'm kind of the A.V. tech now too. Some of those guys can't figure out their own TV remotes, much less complex video equipment."

"I'm proud of you, honey."

"Thanks, Mom."

"Soooo…what was the interview like?"

"Weird. Sherry is this tiny person, like a cross between a bird and a chihuahua. She shows up dressed in attitude—torn jeans, a crop top, and these super-cute knee-high sneakers. Her showmanship is an influencer me-me-me thing. It's painful to watch. And she couldn't sit still to save her soul. If I didn't know better, I'd say she was high."

"You know she wasn't?"

"Well, no. She could've been high, I suppose. But that would be stupid, and she's not stupid."

"What'd she say?"

Diana studied her curry before answering, pushing it around the bowl. "You know, Mom, anything I tell you is confidential, right?" She raised her eyes to meet mine. "I could lose my job. I may even be breaking the law. You can't tell anyone."

"Cross my heart and hope to die," I said, crossing my heart. "This is just for me, honey. I promise. I don't even know who I'd tell."

"Not the ladies at the beauty parlor. Not your catsit people. Not the neighbors. Nobody."

"I swear. This is just between you and me."

Diana leaned forward as if to share a secret.

I said, "Honey, your boob is in the curry."

She pulled back. "Aw damn. This'll never come out."

"Take it off. We'll treat it right away. It'll be fine." I got up to take the shirt from her. She only wore a bra underneath it. "It soaked through to your bra a little too."

"I'm not taking off my bra," Diana said. She picked up a napkin.

"I've seen it all before."

"Ma! This isn't my house. The bra stays."

"Okay, okay. It's not like anyone will ever see that stain anyway."

"Gee, thanks."

"I didn't mean it that way. Look, tell me about Sherry. Spill the beans."

"Well, She showed up with her lawyer, this tall blonde with scary eyes. Nick was practically drooling over her."

"Nick?" I was surprised to discover a touch of jealousy in Diana's tone. I took the shirt to the sink.

"My boss."

"I see. Go on."

"They converged on one of the interview rooms, and Sherry couldn't decide where to sit. She didn't like the chair they assigned her, so the first few minutes was musical chairs until she finally decided to just stand. Well, pace, really. Up and down. Up and down."

"Can we get to the juicy parts, please?"

"If you insist." Diana took a bite of her curry, making me wait even longer. "The night of the fire, she was totally making out with her boyfriend in his car. She didn't even try to spin it. He is, apparently, her alibi. She said that when she noticed that the lights were all out, she figured it was Anthony messing around. But, the most interesting thing she said was that she also thought she saw a 'shadowy figure' lurking outside." She made air quotes around 'shadowy figure.'

That reminded me.

"Oh my god!" I said, dropped the shirt into the sink, and picked up my phone with soapy hands. "I need to show you that video!"

"What video?"

"Mr. Krall sent me a video from the night of the fire. He has security cameras." I wiped one of my hands on my shirt.

"Really? Is there anything in it?"

"Just you watch..." I pulled up the email and opened the attachment. When the video began to play, I moved around the table so Diana and I could watch it together.

As the video began, the Ortizes' house lights were on.

Nothing happened for several minutes.

Diana asked, "Am I missing something?"

In the video, the lights all went out in one fell swoop. The scene was bathed in darkness.

Diana said, "Whoa."

"Yeah," I replied.

"It's too dark," she said.

"Yeah. It was night."

"We can't see anything."

"I know." I exhaled. "I was hoping you could get one of your computer friends to fix it."

"My computer friends? How about me? I'm a tech genius, remember?"

"Oh, right. I keep forgetting." I was only partly kidding. I patted her on the shoulder and was surprised at how warm her bare skin was. It triggered a wave of motherly love. I rested my hand there.

Diana brushed it off. "Let's try it on my laptop," she said, getting up. "Forward me the email." She retrieved her bag and came back with a thin laptop.

I stared at the laptop. "Where'd you get that?"

"Perk of the job," she replied. "I'm very important now, you know?"

I nodded, "I heard you make a mean cup of coffee."

"Not funny, Mom," Diana said, but she was smiling.

Using the laptop helped a lot. Diana worked some magic to lighten the video, and as we watched, a 'shadowy figure' crept around the house from one side to the other, heading toward the back door. Diana zoomed in, and we watched it again in slow motion.

"Is that?" Diana squinted at the screen.

"Manny," I confirmed. "Val was right."

More time passed in the video. Diana and I leaned forward watching for any sign of movement. When it happened, it was a flicker, a dance of light in a downstairs window. The fire had started. Minutes later, Manny ran across the lawn, carrying a bundle in both arms.

"Could that be?" Diana zoomed in on Manny, but it was impossible to see what he was carrying. It looked like an amorphous blob in his arms.

"I don't know," I replied.

"Mom, you need to turn this into the police."

I locked eyes with her, considering the idea.

"Mom? I can give it to them for you."

"No." I waved my hands. "We can't."

"Why not?"

"The reward. If I turn this in, and Manny has the boy, then Val will get the reward. We need more information."

"That's withholding evidence. It's illegal."

"Not if you only withhold it for a little while. Not forever. I just want to talk to Manny first. Confront him with it."

"What if he killed Anthony?"

I had considered the possibility. If Anthony were gone, Manny would inherit the entire fortune in the event of Gregorio and Badahlia's deaths. He might be playing a long game.

I grabbed Diana's forearm. "We should make more copies of it. Just in case he murders me to cover his tracks."

"Mom. You can't be serious."

I clenched my jaw. Bob had always said that 'Stubborn' was my middle name. I needed that reward money. No way I was going to let it go to Val Krall. I said, "I'll just talk to Manny. No big deal. I'll show him the video and see what he says."

Diana stared at me, dead still. She was deciding what to do. I could see the wheels turning in her brain. Finally, she said, "I'm going with you, and we're going to be smart about this. You are *not* allowed to get yourself killed."

"Understood." I gave her a one-armed hug. "We need to go as soon as possible. Can you log in to the police thingy and find out where he lives?"

Diana pushed me off her. "Are you *trying* to get me fired?"

"This is a matter of life and death," I said, using my widened eyes to impress the importance upon her.

"Tomorrow is soon enough, Ma. In the morning, I'll see if I can find out where he lives and works—through regular channels. We can go talk to him at lunchtime—together. Nobody commits murder at lunch."

She had a point.

◆◆◆

◆

Love me, love my cats.

—T-shirt

◆

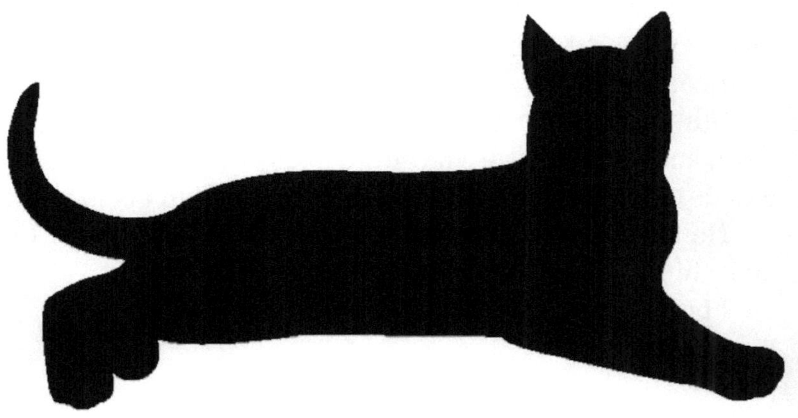

22

MUSE
Is on the hunt.

The mouse got away, leaving me out of breath, with a bruise on my paw and a bloody scratch on the pink of my nose. I'm here to tell you: no piece of tail is worth that. Though it was fun—until the scratch. That burned.

I sat on Greta's front porch, grooming myself. I couldn't let Kitty see me like that. She'd think I was a back-alley Tom. I had a reputation to uphold.

The moon had yet to come out. Darkness blended with my sable fur to make me invisible. I liked it that way. I watched the world, but it couldn't see me. So, when a human man came walking along the sidewalk, I spotted him long before he even knew I existed. Now that's true power. I slipped deeper into the ombre when he came quickly up the walk to the front porch.

He, like me, was covered all in black. He passed within inches of me but didn't notice.

I couldn't differentiate his particular perfume from all the others in the territory—Greta, Greta's humans, Greta's lawn, and Greta's food. The entire house was aromatic with Eau de Greta. Still, his behavior told me he didn't belong.

He snuck up on the front door and stooped down to make himself smaller.

I pounced.

♦ ♦ ♦

23

KITTY
Is in over her head.

"Mrrrrowrrrr!"

I sat straight up in bed. Night had fallen hard, and I'd been sleeping even harder. I stared around, trying to see into the darkness, trying to remember where I was. My heart hammered in my chest.

I opened my ears as wide as they could go and heard the distinct sound of stomping feet.

"Hissssss! Mrrrrowrrr!"

It was out on the porch, below the bedroom window. Instinctively, I reached for my phone.

My fingers were shaking, and it took me several tries to dial Diana.

When she answered, sounding half-asleep, I whispered loudly, "Diana! There's a prowler outside."

"What?"

"A prowler. Outside." I slid out of bed and crept to the side of the window. Pushing the curtain aside, I peeked out at the front lawn. No one was there.

"Mom, are you sure?"

"Yes, I'm sure. They went around to the back. Oh god. Did I remember to lock the back door?"

"Stay calm," Diana said. "Call 911."

"No! You call! You know them. Tell them your mother is in danger!"

"Look, I'm on my way, okay? Go into a room you can lock—like the bathroom—until I get there. Don't turn the lights on."

My neck skin twitched. She had no idea how many times I'd screamed at the TV for the girl hiding from the serial killer to turn the goll-darned lights on. "Hurry!"

I didn't hide in the bathroom—where I'd be cornered—and I didn't leave the lights off. Quite the opposite. I turned them all on. I grabbed the nearest bludgeon—one of Pamela's art pieces—and made plenty of noise as I descended the stairs to the first floor.

"You better get out," I called. "The police are on the way! I'm armed!" I brandished the statue—a phallus-shaped carving in marble—as a warning.

Someone knocked hard on the front door. I jumped and sucked in my breath. The air got stuck in my lungs, and I couldn't make a sound.

When the knock came again, I approached cautiously. When I peered out, I found Diana waiting there. I breathed a sigh of relief and fumbled with the deadbolt.

"Come in! Come in! Hurry! What took you so long?" It had taken her less than five minutes.

Diana squeezed through the crack I left open for her. Muse scooted in on her heels.

I shut and locked the door. "Muse, baby. Are you okay?" I bent to pet him and check him over. He seemed no worse for wear. "What a brave boy."

Muse purred then wandered off to inspect the food dishes.

Diana's attention caught on the phallic statue, and she raised her eyebrows.

I tucked it behind my back.

Diana asked, "Are you okay?"

"I am now. Thank you for coming." I side-stepped to a foyer table and slid the statue into a drawer.

Diana followed me. "Of course, Mom. Do you know who

it was?"

"Probably Manny, coming to kill me. He figured out I have the video. I should call Val!" I reached for my phone, but Diana put her hand over mine.

"No," she said. "It's almost 3am. I'm sure Val is fine. No one is trying to kill you. They came to leave this note on the door." She held out a piece of paper with tape on it. "I pulled it off when I came in."

"What does it say?"

"How should I know?" She thrust it at me.

I took the note and slowly unfolded it. It was a single sheet of printer paper. No lines. Scrawled on it with a fat pink highlighter were the words:

Want the boy back?
I want $500k
by end of day tomorrow.
No cops.
I'll be in touch.

I had to read it twice before my adrenaline-swamped brain understood it. "It's a ransom note."

Diana, who'd been reading over my shoulder, said simply, "Shit. Now we know what happened to Anthony."

A vehicle with its siren blaring approached the house.

In tandem, Diana and I looked toward the window. The flash of red lights was getting brighter.

"You called the cops?" I asked.

"You told me to."

The note felt like a hot potato in my hand. I wanted to throw it. I wanted to hide it. I wanted that reward. I said, "We can't tell them about the note."

"What? Mom."

"It's not our place. That's a decision for the Ortizes to make. It's their child."

We both lowered our voices.

Diana said, "We have to tell the police."

"No. If we tell them, they'll mess it up. There's a boy's life at stake! You and me, we can handle this with...subtlety."

"You and me?" Her deadpan delivery betrayed her skepticism.

"Why not? Look, it says right here. 'No cops.' And they delivered it to me, not to anyone—"

A hard knock shook the front door for the second time that evening. I nearly leapt out of my skin. Then, the doorbell rang, and I almost did it again.

I stared at Diana. She stared at me.

I whispered, "We can go visit the Ortizes bright and early tomorrow. See what they want to do. Okay?"

Diana just stared at me.

"Hello? It's the police. I see you in there. Are you all right?" Of course, he could see us.

I made a 'please don't tell' face at Diana, and she made a frowny face at me. Then, she opened the door. I put the paper inside the waistband of my pajama pants.

"Good evening," said the deputy. "We got a call about a home invasion?"

Diana waved her arm to invite him in. "Mom thought she heard someone on the front porch, Nick," she said, giving me a pointed look.

"That's right!" I said. "I heard them, stomping. I think they attacked my cat."

"Is this your home, ma'am?" Somehow, when that man said it, "ma'am" sounded respectful rather than insulting.

"This is my mom," explained Diana. "She's catsitting here. We live just up the street. She called me first, and I called 911."

The deputy took out a notepad. "Your name, please?" He pointed his pen at me.

"Kitty. Kitty Kats."

The deputy's eyebrows quirked.

Diana said, "She doesn't have dementia. That's really her name."

I had stopped apologizing for it long ago, but Diana still felt the need. "That's Kats with a K. S on the end, not Z." A part of me had always suspected that Diana had been in a hurry to get married so she could change her last name. Sadly, she'd hooked her wagon to someone with an even worse surname.

"So, Mrs. Kats. You're catsitting here, and you heard a prowler outside."

"That's right."

"Okay. I'll take a walk around the outside of the house, and if you'd like, I can check the interior too. Whoever it was will probably have been scared away when they saw me arrive."

My stomach did a flip.

"I'm sure they didn't get inside. If you could just check the outside?"

"Yes, ma'am."

I walked around Diana and opened the door for him. "Thank you, deputy."

The tall, noticeably handsome deputy put his hat back on and headed out the door. When Diana started to follow him, I blocked her with the door, banging into her.

"Ow! What are you doing? I thought I'd—"

I shook my head vigorously and closed the door. Whispering, I said, "What if the kidnapper saw him show up? What if that's the deal-breaker?"

"Mom."

"What if he's out there right now, watching us talk to the cops?"

"Mom."

"What if he's going to kill Anthony now?"

"Mom! Chill! We didn't know about the ransom note

when we called the cops. If the deal is broken, then...there's nothing we can do about it. Let's just do our best and see what happens. It's going to be okay. The kidnapper wants the ransom. They'll do everything in their power to get it."

My heart was racing. That ransom note had made it all so real. Anthony was in danger, real danger, known danger, not just imagined danger. And for some reason, I was the one the kidnapper had chosen to contact.

"That's my boss, by the way," Diana said, pushing the curtains aside to watch the flashlight dance around the corner of the house.

"Really?" I joined her. "He's very attractive."

"Oh? I hadn't noticed."

◆◆◆

24

DIANA
Is a good daughter.

Chief Deputy Nick didn't find anyone hiding in the bushes. Of course. After he had returned to report the all-clear, I accompanied him to his car.

The Ortizes' cat followed me out.

Nick said, "Is that the cat you mentioned? He seems fine."

"Yeah. Thanks for coming so quickly, Boss."

"No problem, Diana. I was up anyway."

"This late?"

"Yeah, old unsolved case rearing its ugly head again. Nothing you need to worry about." He opened the driver-side door and put it between us.

I stood with my hands behind my back.

He said, "You planning to stay here with her tonight?"

I shook my head. "Nah. She'll be fine. She's tougher than she seems."

Nick nodded. "Well, get some rest. 9am is just around the corner."

"What? It's Saturday."

Sad, he said, "Yeah. Until we find the Ortiz kid, it's all hands on deck."

"Aye-aye, Boss." I saluted and then regretted it. I was a goofball.

With a chuckle, Nick got into his car. "I'll see you in a few hours."

"Drive safe."

I watched him go then returned to the Garretts' house.

Mom was waiting for me. "Will you stay here tonight? The guest bed is a queen. Plenty of room for us both. And it's comfortable. We can get a few hours sleep, then go see the Ortizes."

I told her, "I can't leave Mimi home alone."

Worry creased Mom's brow. "At least stay until I fall asleep? If I'm here alone..."

"Sure. I can do that."

She brightened immediately and led the way. She got in under the covers, and I lay down on top of them.

"Good night," she said. "Thanks, honey."

"You're welcome, Mom."

I waited...and before long, I fell into a deep sleep.

♦♦♦

25

MUSE
Is annoyed.

I did not sleep a wink that night. Not a winken. Not a blinken. Not a nod. I patrolled the perimeter of the house, keeping my keen eyes and ears perked for the prowler to return. I still had the taste of his blood on my tongue from where I'd licked it off my claws. He had not seen my attack coming. I'm just that good.

I'd have gone for his throat next, but he took my warning and fled. I did not expect him to return but neither was I going to let down my guard.

I was annoyed. I'd wanted to get his scent so I could recognize him.

I sniffed and sniffed, and sneezed.

♦♦♦

◆

**And this mess is so big
And so deep and so tall,
We cannot pick it up.
There is no way at all!**

—Dr. Seuss, The Cat in the Hat

◆

26

KITTY
Solves problems.

Diana's snoring woke me. It was the crack of dawn when I rolled to sit on the edge of the bed. My eyes felt like wet marshmallows and my mouth tasted like ash. I retrieved the ransom note from my bedside table and read it again...and again. It was real. I hadn't dreamed it. I hadn't imagined it. I was holding, in my hot little hand, a real ransom note.

"Wake up, Di," I said, bouncing the mattress. "We need to go see the Ortizes."

Diana grumbled and tried to bury her head under the pillow.

I got up and began removing my pajamas. "Do you know where they're staying?"

The answer came as an unintelligible mumble.

I'd folded my clothes from the day before and put them on a chair. Whenever I did an overnight, I waited until I was back home during the day to shower and change clothes. Since I had to go home every day anyway, it just made the clean-up easier. I liked to leave my employers' home better than I found it, with no traces of me anywhere.

Once I was dressed, I said, "C'mon, honey. Get up. I'm going down to feed Greta. Use the bathroom if you need to, and I'll make coffee."

Diana moaned.

The house looked much less scary in the light of day, and I was glad to have survived the night. Greta came out of her plush kitty bed and followed me to the kitchen.

"Good morning, Greta. How are you, honey? Were you bothered by all the chaos last night? I'm so sorry that happened. Let's get you some breakfast, okay? There's a good girl."

Greta—much to my surprise—rubbed against my ankle.

"Good girl! Thank you, Greta." I purred at her—literally. "Prrrrr." When speaking to kitties, it's best to use kitty language along with human language. "That was very sweet. You must be hungry. I'll get it right now." My rolling monologue with kitties varied little. I told them they were good, beautiful, and loved. I talked to them in soft, warm tones to put them at ease. It was one of my strategies to get them to identify me as a friend. And it usually worked.

I washed and filled her water dish then did the same with the food plate. She dove right in, face first. My stomach grumbled, and I realized I was hungry too. "Surviving prowlers is hungry work, isn't it, sweetpea? Good girl."

At about that time, Diana came thumping down the stairs. She moved like a zombie, eyes only half open. "Two minutes to coffee," I promised, hurrying over to set up the machine. It was one of those pod contraptions.

Apparently, I was putting the pod in upside down, because Diana appeared at my side and said, "Let me." She used her hip to push me away. I watched as she put the pod in the right way then added more water to the reservoir. She dug a mug out of the cabinet and placed it on the platform. In sixty seconds, she had the coffee brewing.

"You want one?" she asked.

"Yes, please. Toast?"

"Yes, please."

I wanted the loaf of bread I'd left on the counter, but it wasn't where I thought I'd put it. I looked in the fridge. Sometimes I put the bread there. It wasn't there.

"Sorry, no bread." I checked the garbage. It wasn't there

either. "I swear I had a loaf of bread. You don't think the prowler actually got in last night, do you?"

"And stole your bread?"

I shrugged. It was plausible. "He was hungry?"

"Mom, it's more likely that you used the last of it, or it's in your car, or it's still at the grocery store."

I couldn't deny that things like that happened to me, and not because I'm getting old; it's always been like that. Bob used to call me the absent-minded professor. Trivialities slipped through the cracks.

I said, "We can eat something when we get home. I need to shower and change clothes anyway, before we go to the Ortizes. You do know where they're staying, right?"

Diana's coffee was done. She offered it to me.

I shook my head. "You need it more than I do."

Closing her eyes, Diana took a deep inhalation of the steam from her mug.

I said, "Di? You *do* know where they are, yes?"

"They're at a cushy B&B on Oceanview."

"Excellent." I shuffled off to scoop the litter box, and Diana set up the machine for my coffee to brew. I called from the mudroom, "Oh, good girl! You left me presents!"

"Excuse me?" called Diana.

"I'm talking to Greta!"

After reminding me twenty times that she only had an hour before she had to be at work, Diana offered to drive. Freshly dressed, I hurried out to her car to wait for her— and hopefully encourage her to hurry a bit. She had already walked Mimi while I was showering, but it wasn't always easy to tear her away from her baby. If she could take the pup into work with her, she wouldn't hesitate. Speaking of babies, I hadn't seen Muse yet that morning and was worried about him. He hadn't seemed hurt when he came into the Garrett house after the prowler scare, but the sound of him yowling haunted me.

I was already growing attached to the little tuxedo cat. My instincts told me he was special.

I hadn't noticed him going outside, but he could have slipped back out when the deputy left. Just to cover my bases, I'd left food and water on the porch and extra inside for him, so he wouldn't go hungry or thirsty. To my knowledge, he'd never been an indoor-only cat, so I figured he could handle himself in the neighborhood.

I watched the scenery of Wyrdwood scroll by. The beauty never ceased to amaze me. The Pacific Ocean, the gradual rise of the land, the tall hills further inland, the national forest, the abundance of evergreens and flowering trees. No matter where you looked, Wyrdwood was magickally gorgeous. And the residents took great pride in their town. They kept their own parcels of land clean, and they policed their neighbors as well.

That got me thinking. I asked, "Do you think Mr. Krall might have video of last night's prowler?"

"Hm," Diana replied. "Unless he *was the prowler. Did you hear a car drive away?*"

"No."

She put on her blinker. "Whoever it was must have been on foot, at least for a block or so. That means it could've been a neighbor, or they could've parked down the street."

"What about a bicycle?"

"Uh uh. Too conspicuous. Besides, what kidnapper is going to ride a bicycle to drop off a ransom note?"

My phone rang. I looked to see who it was then answered, "Sherry?"

"Yeah, it's me. You called about a job?" Her voice was surprisingly mellow and pleasing to the ear, though her manner was abrupt.

"I did. This is Kitty Kats, and I live down the street from the Ortizes. I need someone to walk my dog sometimes."

"How big is it?"

"About the size of your pinkie toe." I looked over at Diana, anticipating the sour look she threw my way.

"Okay, sure. How much?"

"Ten bucks for a fifteen-minute walk and poop pickup if she makes any?"

"The lowest I could go is fifteen if there's poop involved."

"Deal. How about Monday, Wednesday, and Friday after you get out of school?"

"Okay, sure."

"Do you have transportation?"

"My boyfriend does. He can come with me, yeah?"

"No problem. Do you do a lot of jobs like this?"

"I guess. I also work part time at Sprinkles, the ice cream shop down by the marina."

"I know it well."

Sherry suddenly sounded grown up. "You do what you gotta do, I suppose. I'm saving up for college."

"That's industrious of you. Do you know what you want to study?"

"Obstetrics."

"Really?"

"Yeah, sure. The birth process is so fire. And helping other women, well, it's kind of my calling. Way I figure it, I better save up now while I'm still living with the 'rents—and not paying rent."

I felt younger just talking to her. "That's a smart move. Say, can I ask you a question?"

"I guess. About what?"

"The night of the fire at the Ortizes, do you remember if the candle was lit before or after the lights went out?"

"There was no candle burning when I was inside."

"Okay, but you noticed the candle?"

"Huh?"

"Did you see a small light come back on?"

"I was kinda busy."

"Think hard. What do you remember about the lights going out?" I shifted the phone to my other ear.

"I remember…the whole house went dark at once. There was no candle light. It was pitch black."

"Okay."

"That's all I remember."

"Well done. Thank you. I'll see you tomorrow at my place? I'll text you the address."

"Okay, sure. See ya." She hung up before I had a chance to answer, and it bugged me like when people didn't sign their texts. I knew—mentally—that you didn't need to sign your texts, but *emotionally, I still hadn't gotten over the idea that you were supposed to put a signature after a note or letter. Boomer.*

As soon as I hung up and put my phone away, Diana asked, "Why are you hiring someone to walk my dog?"

"I'm not. You are. Because you don't want her pooping in the foyer ever again. It's bad for her morale and mine. Face it, honey, now that you're working, you won't be able to spend as much time with Mimi. You will probably want to add Tuesday and Thursday too."

Diana sighed like the burdened daughter she was.

I asked, "Are we there yet?"

◆◆◆

◆

**God's grace = Magick.
Amen.
Discuss.**

*—Minister Brine's shortest sermon,
left on a whiteboard
at the Wyrdwood Universalist Church.
(He had a funeral to attend.)*

◆

27

KITTY
Stumbles into a pocket dimension.

The C'mon Inn, the bed-and-breakfast where the Ortizes were staying, had a modern style. A perfect square, it had smooth outside wall panels and windows designed for maximum illumination and symmetry. It sat back from the road, a rambling alien ship tucked in amidst Nature. Cherry trees covered in pink blossoms lined the driveway and added whimsical softness to the landscaping and surrounding forest.

We pulled into a spot close to the front.

"Their car is here," I said, pointing out the red convertible.

"This place looks out of sync with our world," Diana said, leaning on the steering wheel and peering upward at the facade.

I grabbed my tote bag and opened the car door to get out. "Let's go in."

Wide stairs took us up to the porch. It was more a platform than a porch, with a potted plant as the only decor. The front door had a tiny, unobtrusive OPEN sign glowing pink in the window, so I pushed down the handle and entered.

My first impression said there was more space inside than outside. And, there were no corners. Every edge was smoothed. A cathedral ceiling with rounded beams arched over our heads, making the reception foyer airy and bright. It reminded me of a building designed by Gaudi or a giant beehive.

A large gas fireplace served as a natural intersection between four quadrants where people could relax. Each section had chairs and/or couches, all mid-century chic with varying levels of comfort. An oval buffet along one wall offered breakfast options kept warm in stainless steel. The room smelled of cinnamon, honey, and vanilla.

"Wow!" whispered Diana. "Pocket dimension?"

Taking it all in, I replied, "That would be my guess."

"I've never been in one before."

"Me either." Instinctively, I reached for Diana's hand and clasped it. Pocket dimensions were ancient and rare, sometimes dangerous. The rules of physics could be different, topsy-turvy, or even beyond the comprehension of someone who has lived in Reality all their lives. Most often, they're jealously guarded by a certain line of kin who "owns" it. The owners of this one had chosen to turn theirs into a bed-and-breakfast for wealthy clients. People like me and Diana—regular folk—hardly ever saw this level of magick in their entire lives. I felt like a kid who had accidentally stumbled into Disney World.

"May I help you?" asked a woman with plump curves. She was petite, even shorter than me, and—if I had to guess—in her fifties? She had white hair piled upon her head to give her a bit more height, and her eyes were huge in her face—a vibrant green. "I'm afraid we don't have any vacancies at this time," she added when we didn't immediately respond. Her voice was breathy and soprano.

I gathered my wits and approached her with a smile. "We're looking for the Ortizes. It was my understanding that they're staying here? We need to speak with them, please."

The woman ran her fingertips along her jaw as if stroking an invisible beard. "Ortizes. I'll have to check my records. If you would please be so kind as to wait, I'll be right back. If you'd like some coffee, please help yourself."

"Thank you," I told her.

She nodded, pushed on a wall panel that turned out to be an obfuscated swinging door, and disappeared inside.

Diana and I made wide-eyed looks at each other, simultaneously.

"I'm going for some coffee," Diana said, freeing her hand from mine. She turned sharply and headed for the drink buffet.

"Wait." I followed her. Keeping my voice low, I said, "You know what they say about drinking or eating in other dimensions."

"It'll be fine." She dismissed me with a wave of her hand. "This is a business. They're not going to poison their clientele." She pulled a ceramic mug from the tray. "You want some?"

My stomach was *not* up to both a pocket dimension and coffee, so I shook my head.

The woman eventually came out through the same swinging door and walked all the way across the lobby with a slow, elegant gait. The trip took her so long that Diana and I started to meet her halfway before she could get to us.

She waited until everyone had stopped moving then asked, "May I have your names? Mr. Ortiz would like to know who's calling."

I replied, "Please tell Mr. Ortiz that his neighbors Kitty and Diana Kats are here, and that it's urgent that we speak to him. It has to do with his son." I wished I'd said all that earlier. It would have saved us time, but who could have predicted that this woman was slower than a sloth swimming upstream.

"I will relay this information. Please make yourselves comfortable."

"Thank you." I put my hand in my tote to make sure the note was still there. It was.

Diana and I sat in strange round chairs that molded to your body and were far more difficult to get out of than into. We watched several couples, groups, and individuals come through the lobby for coffee, breakfast, or to make their way back to the "real" world. They all had that well-put-together look of the rich and maybe famous. Some let their disguise down and showed their natural forms—elven mostly, some fae. The elves were tall, elegant, and relatively attractive, while the fae came in all shapes and sizes—literally. The one thing they had in common was their pointy ears. Whether long or short, the pointed tips gave them away, and the little green monster of envy stirred in my chest. It made them so intriguing. Quite often, the feature carried over to their human guises. My ears were big, round, and crooked. One sat higher on my head than the other. I kicked myself whenever I reflexively tucked my hair behind them.

Fortunately, Diana had inherited her father's ears—small, even, and with a slight point at the tip.

A posh orcneas came through. He looked like he was ready to play golf. He resembled my neighbor Mike only in physical form. I'd have bet money he hadn't mowed a single blade of grass in his entire life.

The B&B's patrons laughed loudly and carried on about tennis or boarding schools or how they planned to spend the summer in France.

Several studied me and Diana—my well-loved non-Gucci tote bag, Diana's torn jeans, and our wind-blown hair. I found myself sinking deeper into my chair. Whether it was a facade or not, Diana neither noticed nor cared that they were scrutinizing us and finding us lacking.

"They're wondering why we're here," I whispered.

"Who?"

"All these wealthy people."

"Y'think?" Diana looked boldly back at them. "Ignore them."

"They're all kith," I said.

"Duh. You think they'd let Normals in here? No freakin' way. That may even be illegal. I'd guess anyone without the spark sees a CLOSED sign on the door."

A newlywed couple arrived and were helped at the front desk by a tall, suited man with slicked-back hair, a neatly trimmed beard, and eyes so beady they were practically non-existent. He wore glasses that dominated his face.

The couple couldn't keep their hands off one another.

Diana watched them with tension in her jaw and eyes. I could almost read the thoughts going through her mind. She was remembering her own honeymoon, her husband, and his catastrophic betrayal. My heart ached for her. I reached out and grabbed her hand again.

"So," she said, dragging her attention off the newlyweds. "What was all that about the candle?"

"That was the babysitter. I wanted to know if Anthony had lit the candle before the lights went out. Some people are saying he was the one who threw the switch in the fuse-box. If he was, then I figure he'd have lit a candle first." I crossed my legs at the knee. "It's not proof of his guilt, but it would help."

"So, did he?"

I looked around to see who might be listening then leaned forward and lowered my voice. "I don't think so. She didn't remember seeing the candle lit, and she said it was pitch black when the lights went out. So, there was no candle burning then. Little Anthony probably lit the candle after the lights went out."

"That's good thinking, Mom."

"Thanks, honey."

"Have you thought about what you're going to tell the Ortizes?"

"Yes," I replied slowly, "I'll just give them the note, explain how I got it, and tell them I'll help them. I don't know more than that."

"Are you going to discourage them from calling the police?"

"Well..." I was, of course, but I didn't want to say so. If they called the police, I could kiss the reward goodbye. I pointedly turned my eyes to an elegant, older pair of men.

Diana followed my gaze to them and whispered, "They're handsome."

I nodded. My ploy to derail the topic of the police had worked.

She asked, "You ever wonder what it'd be like to date again?"

"I think they're gay, honey."

Diana laughed. "Obvi," she said. "But it might do you good to get out. Let a man pamper you a bit. You're still hot."

"Bite your tongue!" I said a bit too loudly.

"You are—when you don't smell like kitty litter."

"I smell like kitty litter?"

"Only sometimes. Pine, mostly. It's not entirely unpleasant."

"Oh my god."

"It's not like you smell like cat pee. Just...the litter."

"I can't help it! I get that dust all over me."

"I know."

"Kitty," said a man. "What are you doing here?"

"Gregorio." I leapt to my feet—or, I would have leapt to my feet if the chair hadn't had a suction hold on my butt. I wiggled and grunted, and finally, Diana had to help me up. I was half-expecting to hear a pop as I pulled my bottom free.

"Gregorio," I said again, trying to regain some semblance of dignity. I glanced around. There were still a number of people lingering, eating, and moving through the lobby. "Is there a place where we can speak in private?"

"What's this about?" he asked.

I lowered my voice. "It's about your son. I received a

ransom note."

"What?" Both the tone and volume of Gregorio's response drew all eyes in the room to us.

I reached into my tote bag and produced the note. Without a word, I handed it to him.

The blood drained from Gregorio's tanned face.

♦♦♦

◆

**When you hate,
You are hateful.
When you love,
You are beloved.**

*—sign in the window at
the Prose, Poetry, and Poe
bookshop in Wyrdwood*

◆

28

MUSE
Finds treasure.

Dirt and I have a special relationship. Many people think cats are prissy, but the truth is that we love dirt. It's great for hiding our poop and for rolling in when it's hot outside. It often holds treasures, like ground squirrels, moles, mice, and antiques.

Being no ordinary cat—need I remind, I *am* the King of Cats in exile—I had an appreciation for the ancient and not-so-ancient secrets that are hidden in dirt. Thus it was that, when I saw Little Manny Big Man digging around the yard, I guessed what he was doing. I'd been aware of his scheme for some time, actually. He'd be so furious to know that I'd been digging up the gold he'd buried, almost before the dust settled. It gave me a rush of smug satisfaction to watch his frustration grow as he poked through the grass and kicked rocks over, looking for his markers. Meanwhile, I had a pile of stolen artifacts hidden behind a rusty old watering can in the garden shed.

Manny had been pilfering from his family for years. Small things, always. A ceramic figurine here. A silver spoon there. The man either had an obsession—or a long-tail plan.

Personally, I didn't blame him. His brother, Gregorio, could have shared the inheritance with him once the old goat was dead. However, Gregorio was nothing if not greedy. The man wanted his treats and to eat them too.

It was with great anticipation that I observed Manny. He rambled around a spot where an item still remained, but I had batted his marker halfway across the lawn. I was rooting for him to find it.

Manny had always been kind to me in that condescending way humans do, speaking to me as if I were a kitten. Occasionally, he had paid me homage with a brief petting. And *he* had never tossed me out of the house into the rain.

Disappointment hung over us both when Manny finally gave up on finding his treasure. He wrapped his arms around himself and walked back to his car. He was a hobo, a vagabond, a stray. Exiled, like me, from his home. I felt his pain, and one day—maybe—I would give him back his gold.

Once he'd driven away, I scratched at the dirt over the item. A flicker of white appeared. I kept at it.

Ultimately, the earth revealed a skull. A human skull.

I hissed, and my hackles all went up.

But, it was tiny. As small as my own would be. It had a long black growth emerging from the back and a giant hole in the top. It was encased in clear plastic.

Once my alarm had passed, I scratched the skull out and picked it up in my teeth. It wasn't too heavy. It tasted of tobacco. I carried it to the garden shed and added it to my stash of loot.

◆◆◆

29

KITTY
Learns TMI about the Ortizes.

Gregorio did not look well. He asked, "Why you?"

I told him, "It was just random. I just happened to be catsitting at the Garrett's. Putting the note on a neighbor's front door is a convenient way to deliver it. It's less risky than trying to get it directly to you."

"You've put some thought into this."

"Yes. It's what I do."

"Did you call the police?"

"No," I replied meeting Diana's gaze. "And we're not going to."

"Good."

"What are you going to do?"

"I have to call my wife." Gregorio moved toward the front door of the B&B and exited.

We followed.

My ears popped as I crossed the threshold back into Reality. The scent of cherry blossoms filled the air.

Gregorio stood on the front lawn and spoke into his cell. "There's a ransom note. Some asshole has my son." He shifted the phone to his other ear and wiped his eyes. "Half a mil." He paused then, "No. It's not her. She wouldn't do this."

Diana and I shamelessly eavesdropped.

"That makes no sense. He was taken before I asked for the divorce." He paced across the freshly mown grass, getting little bits stuck to his fancy shoes. "I'm telling you, there's no way she could've known."

"What if," whispered Diana, "Gregorio is staging this to keep this money out of the divorce?"

I squinted at the man. "You think he's that good an actor?"

"Maybe?"

Gregorio said, "Are you at the office?"

"I think you should go to work," I told Diana.

"And miss this?"

Facing her, I latched onto her forearm. I kept my voice low and enunciated the best I could. "You can't afford to lose this job in your first week. Besides, I need you to look into Val Krall."

"I already tried. There's not much online about him."

"Try harder. He's got a grudge against them and is just pompous enough to want to teach them a parenting lesson. Good intentions, bad execution. When I was there, I saw a photo of Val with a boy. Can you find out if he has a son?"

"What are you going to do? I'm your ride."

"I'll go with him to tell his wife. I'm in this now, up to my armpits."

"Just don't get in over your head, Mom."

"I won't."

Gregorio was about to hang up. "I'm coming in to the office. Yes. See you soon, my love."

"Go," I gave Diana a little push. "I'll call you later."

With a dour look, Diana said, "Don't do anything ridiculous, okay?"

"Not my style."

"Yes, it is." Diana went to her car.

Gregorio was just coming back to me. "Where's *she* going?"

"She has to go to work. I'll tag along with you." I smiled. "You don't mind, do you? Badahlia may have some questions for me about what happened."

He couldn't argue with my logic.

As we got into the fancy red car, he studied me again and then asked, "Why *you?*"

All I could do was shrug.

Gregorio and Badahlia worked at the Ortiz Law Firm, a company founded by Gregorio's grandfather. Ownership remained in the family, but it was run by a board of directors. Gregorio led me in through the front doors and past a parade of people who all wished him a good morning.

I did my best to smooth down my hair after the ride in the convertible as we headed for the elevators.

Gregorio pushed the UP button.

A woman—a brunette with high cheekbones and a tight-fitting herring-bone suit—joined us there. They didn't look at one another, but Gregorio said, "Does she know I'm coming?"

"I didn't tell her," answered the woman, pretending to ignore him. "Are you nuts?"

"I often wonder," Gregorio answered. He'd forgotten I was there too. Focusing on the elevator doors, he said, "I told the police about us."

"Why?"

"You're my alibi. I told them we were together at your place. All night."

The elevator arrived, and we all got into it. I made myself as small as possible so they'd forget me more. The woman was obviously the *other* woman, and it sure sounded like Gregorio was feeding her notes on what to say to the police.

"The police will probably be calling you in," Gregorio continued, dropping all pretense and touching the woman's hair.

The elevator bell rang, and Gregorio and the woman turned toward the doors. "After you," Gregorio said, indicating the woman should pass ahead. He did not extend me the same courtesy.

I followed them into a wide, window-lined office cluster with a half-moon reception desk.

"Good morning, Mr. Ortiz," said the man behind the desk.

"Is my wife—"

Badahlia came charging into view. "You!" She pointed at the brunette. "You're fired. Get out of my sight!"

The brunette raised both hands and backed away.

With a glare, Badahlia turned on her husband. "I've contacted H.R. I don't want to see her here anymore."

Gregorio said, "We need to talk somewhere private."

"I suppose you're living with her now?"

"No. I'm not. Don't bring this into the office—"

"Me?" Badahlia's eyes sparked. "You're the ones who just waltzed in here together."

Gregorio had the good grace to look sorry. "Listen, we need to talk. It has to do with Anthony."

"Ant'ony?" Badahlia's whole demeanor changed. Her eyes grew wide and afraid. "What have you heard?"

"Let's go into your office."

"Did they find him?" Badahlia's body shrank and began to shake.

"No. Let's go in—"

"Just tell me, goddammit!" Her entire body clenched.

"There's been a ransom note," Gregorio said, deadpan. He made no move to comfort his wife but did take her by the shoulders and directed her toward the office.

I followed them.

Gregorio cast an apologetic look at his other woman as he shut the door.

As if in shock, Badahlia noticed me for the first time. "Kitty? What are you doing here?"

I handed that baton to Gregorio. He still had the ransom

note in his pocket, and he produced it to show her. "Someone left that on Kitty's front door."

"Not *my* door," I tried to clarify, but it didn't matter. No one was listening to me.

Badahlia's face melted. "They want the money by tomorrow night?"

"No," I said. "I think they mean by tonight. I actually received the note last night."

"Last night?" Badahlia's eyes grew wide and wild. "Why are we just hearing about this now? Oh my god!"

I put up my hands to calm her. "It was about 3am. Technically, I suppose that's today. So it could be tomorrow night."

Gregorio said, "We'll have it ready today. Just in case that's what they meant. I'll call the bank and arrange it."

"You need to do that right away," said Badahlia, urgency in her tone. "They probably won't have that kind of cash."

Gregorio took out his phone and walked across the hall to a conference room. He closed the door behind him.

When I looked back at Badahlia, she was staring at me. "Why you?"

"The kidnapper left the note on the Garrett's front door. I'm catsitting for them while they're in Hawaii."

Badahlia paced behind her desk. She put her palm to her forehead and closed her eyes to stop the tears that had arisen.

I waited. Any thought I'd had that she was behind the kidnapping flew right out the window. No way she was that good an actor. She was a terrified mother. No ifs, ands, or buts about it.

"I'm sorry this is happening," I told her.

She pinched her lips together and nodded, unable to speak.

Gregorio came back. "The bank says they can help us, but there's going to be a fee."

"So?" Badahlia threw her arms up. "This is our *son!*"

"I know, I know. I told them to go ahead. I'm going to pick up the money this afternoon."

Badahlia asked, "They said they'd be in touch. Does that mean they'll call?"

Gregorio looked to me for the answer.

I shook my head and widened my eyes. "I don't know. I guess we just wait and see."

The waiting was torture. The longer Badahlia and Gregorio spent in the same room, the more tense it became. I had to get some air, so I excused myself to go find the restroom. It was just an excuse. I wandered in the direction I'd seen the brunette go.

She was in a small block of cubicles, cleaning out her desk, and mumbling to herself.

"I'm sorry you lost your job," I said, though I kind of wasn't. Sleeping with a married man—strike one. Sleeping with a coworker—strike two. And sleeping with the husband of your boss—strike three, you're out. She'd been doomed from the moment she first smiled at Gregorio. "I'm sure you'll have no trouble finding a new one."

"Oh, it's okay," the brunette—Janette Beck according to her nameplate—replied. "I'll be fine. This job sucked anyway."

I ran my finger along the top of her cubicle wall. "How about this kidnapping, huh?"

"Yeah. Poor kid. He's so sweet. He must be terrified."

I briefly wondered whether we were talking about the same kid then said, "I don't suppose you have any theories about who might have taken him?"

"Pirates?"

I thought she was joking and almost chuckled. I had to swallow it when I realized she was dead serious.

Janette put a stack of picture frames into a cardboard

printer-paper box. "It happens all the time, abroad."

"Mm. You can't think of anyone more personal? Anyone who might have it in for the Ortizes?"

Janette had an animated way of expressing herself. Her facial expressions went from surprised to earnest in a heartbeat. "Only his mother. Badahlia is ruthless. If she thought she could stop Gregorio from divorcing her, or if she thought she could get more of his money, then she'd totally do it. She's a shark. I was up for a promotion, and she talked shit about me to the head of the company. Got it rescinded. I didn't even think she knew about me and Gregorio, but last week—same day I lost the promotion to that dipshit Kenneth—she made it her business to let me know *she* was responsible and why."

"Oh no!" I said. "That must've been terrible. What did she say?" I counted back the days. The lost promotion had happened before the fire.

"She said she was sorry—not sorry—about the promotion, and that the pain of losing it couldn't compare to the pain of losing her husband." Janette's frown deepened. "She must have found out about me and him."

"I see. So how long have you and Gregorio been an item?"

"Almost a year."

My phone started ringing. It was an unknown number. Probably a robot telemarketer. I used it as an excuse to leave though. "I have to take this," I said. "Good luck."

"Hey," Janette called as I left the cubicle. "I wouldn't be surprised if she had a detective following us."

I nodded, pointed at my phone, then answered it for verisimilitude. "Hello?"

A man's robotic voice said, "Is this the catsitter?"

He had all my attention.

"Yes."

"Do you have the money?"

"We're getting it."

"Good."

"Take the money to the house where you're catsitting. Wait for my next call. You and only you will deliver it. Or else what happens next will be your fault. Got it?"

"How will I—"

The kidnapper hung up on me.

♦♦♦

◆

**There is no "I"
In Good.
There *is* in Evil.
Make good choices.**

*—from Principal Maina's commencement speech
Wyrdwood North High School, 2022*

◆

30

DIANA
Meets a handsome stranger.

Mom called me after speaking to the kidnapper. She told me what they'd said, and I encouraged her to go to the police. Of course, she refused. I thought about doing it myself, but I'd have been betraying both her and the Ortizes. Their plan to hand over the ransom seemed wise. I'd done some research online—sketchy, I know—and the internet said that most kidnappers returned the victim, if paid. For all I knew, kidnappers could have created those web pages, but whatever. I took hope from it, and I kept my mouth shut.

She said, "Don't call me until I say it's okay. I don't want to tie up this line and risk missing the kidnapper's call. Okay?"

"You better call *me,*" I said, "the moment you hear from them. Okay?"

"If I can't call, I'll text. I'll let you know what they want me to do."

"You want me to stay over with you again tonight? I can go with you to deliver the money. I can drive."

"No. That might spook them. I'll be fine. The Ortizes will give me the money later this afternoon, I think, and I'll text you when I get back to the Garrett's house with it."

"Okay."

"Don't worry."

"Right. My mother is going to deliver a ransom to kidnappers, and I'm not supposed to worry."

"I'll be fine."

"You better. And call me as soon as you hear from them again."

"I'll text. I promise."

"And Mom?"

"Yes?"

"You're not the kidnapper, are you?"

"Shhh...the walls have ears."

She laughed. I laughed.

"I love you, Mom."

"I love you too, honey."

An uneasy queasiness started up in my stomach.

The sheriff's department was making no progress in its investigation. The parents—either one or both—were the prime suspects. The sheriff himself had returned from his fishing trip and taken an interest. Sheriff Frank Metzger favored Badahlia. He had subpoenaed phone records for them both and discovered that Gregorio had called his wife's office at least once a day. To the sheriff, that meant he was a good husband. I chose not to remind him that Gregorio's mistress worked at the same place. Staying off the sheriff's radar seemed like a smart move.

As soon as I'd arrived at work, I'd tackled that photo Nick had given me. No matter how I tried to make it clearer, I couldn't do it, so I was happily cyber-stalking Manny Ortiz and Val Krall when a man-shaped shadow stretched across my desk. I quickly switched to a different window and accidentally opened the window with the cute leggings shop I'd been browsing. I had to switch again.

My visitor's aroma reached me. Forest. Evergreens and fresh air. It was far from unpleasant. I closed my eyes and took a deep breath. Christmas. He smelled like Christmas.

"Diana Kats?" he said by way of greeting. His voice saying my name was to my ears like butterscotch pudding was to my tongue.

"That's my name," I said without the usual sass. I rotated slowly in my chair and lifted my gaze to take him in. "Ask me again and I'll tell you the same." I liked the sight of him.

Tall and buff, he had to be a body builder, and his stance was lazy. About my age, maybe a little older, he had the slightest shine of silver already streaking his dark hair. His skin was tanned by his ancestry and buffed by the sun. He crossed his arms and ignored my witty retort. "How much spark do you have?"

"Excuse me?" *Spark* was a codeword for having magick in one's blood. The more spark, the more you were aware of the 'paranormal' races. Para, a Greek prefix meaning *alongside* or *beyond*. Technically, spark was unquantifiable. You had it or you didn't, and there were no units of measure.

"How much spark do you have?" he repeated. It was like asking a lady how old she was but much worse. It may even have been illegal for me to answer, depending on who was asking.

"I can be sparky. Why?"

"I got none."

"And yet you know enough to ask me that question."

"Yes. I need your help." His lips tightened as if he hated even saying the words.

"*My* help? I'm sorry. Who are you?"

"Eagle Crenshaw. I'm a P.I."

"Seriously?" I pushed my chair back and stood. The top of my head only came up to his chin, and I'm not petite like my mom is. I have Dad to thank for that.

He barely blinked, meeting my gaze. "Seriously. I've got a missing person. I need someone who knows the people involved and who has the spark. Your mother suggested you."

"My mother?" I studied him, his dark earnest eyes and the tick in his jaw when he unconsciously clenched one side of his teeth. He nodded once, succinct. I asked, "You looking for the kid?"

Eagle nodded again.

Crossing my arms, I leaned on my desk. "Tell me more."

"I've got my eye on a suspect, but there's shit going down—pardon my French—that isn't human."

My eyebrows lifted. He also didn't seem like the kind of man who avoided foul language, so the apology signaled respect, which I appreciated. As long as he didn't call me 'ma'am,' we'd get along just fine.

His jeans were stained with oil and scuffed. His shoes—large, steel-toed, and well-worn—had the kind of sole that made him a full inch taller. His t-shirt was emblazoned with a microbrewery logo, and to top it all off, he wore one of those armored leather jackets that bikers wear. The hem hit him just right at his narrow hips and enhanced the breadth of his shoulders.

When my gaze returned to his face, he had a small smile playing there. He'd noticed me checking him out. I mean, how could he have missed it?

I had to admit, I was intrigued. "I'm listening."

"Not here," Eagle said, and for the first time, he revealed his discomfort at being in the police department. He glanced around the room without moving his head, only his eyes. "Can you come for coffee? Tea? Whiskey? Whatever you drink?"

"It's eleven o'clock in the morning."

"And?"

"I could eat."

"Lunch, then. Good."

"You buying?"

"Yeah." Eagle turned toward the exit as if the matter were settled.

I locked my computer, grabbed my jacket and backpack, and followed him. The view from that angle was pretty good too.

Eagle drove a Saab, one of the most inconspicuous—and comfortable—cars around. He opened my door first—which was nice—but didn't wait around to close it once I was in, which also was nice. Manners without condescension. Score one for Eagle.

The interior of the car was much neater than I expected. It had a plastic garbage can in the backseat, half-full, and a mini-fridge plugged into the cigarette lighter. I immediately started playing with buttons, and when Eagle got in, he said, "Careful. You never know which one is the ejector."

I laughed.

We put on our seatbelts, and he started the car.

The buttons for locks and windows were intuitive, but I wasn't finding the one I wanted.

I asked, "Can you warm my butt, please."

Eagle tried to hide a smile but didn't even miss a beat. "Sure." He pushed the button to turn on the seat warmer as he pulled out of the parking spot. Immediately, I felt the heat flow across my bottom and up my lower back. I let out a sigh and relaxed.

"You live in your car?" I asked.

"Sometimes."

The thought occurred to me that I was in the vehicle of a stranger, possibly a serial killer, and I didn't care. The seat warmers were worth it. "If you're taking me out to the woods to kill me, thanks for doing it in this car."

"It makes you more malleable," he said without hesitation.

I huffed a surprised laugh and cast him a sideways glance to catch the sparkle in his eye. He was joking. Of course, he was. "Where we going?"

"I know a little diner just off the coastal highway. This time of day, it won't be too busy. It serves American comfort food. You okay with that?"

"Sounds right up my alley. So, why don't you tell me what's going on?"

He nodded, glanced at me, then looked back to the road. "I been following this dude. Manny Ortiz. The missing kid's uncle, father's brother. He's been acting weird."

"Weird how?"

"Going out to their house—or what's left of it—in the middle of the night and searching around the lawn with a flashlight."

"Why?"

"No idea. That's what I'm hoping you can help me with. After he left, I poked around. All I found were small spots where the turf had been dug up. And cat poop."

I managed to hide my laugh behind a cough. "Maybe he's a feline shifter?" I was playing with him. Feline shifters don't leave their poop lying around people's lawns.

"See, that's why I need you. I'm pretty sure Manny Ortiz is up to no good. I need you to look at it and tell me if you see anything unnatural."

"Look at what? The cat poop?"

"Yes. No. The lawn."

"What are you expecting to find?"

"I don't know. Motive. Evidence. Maybe he's out there trying to cover up clues that implicate him. Clues that I can't see because I'm normal."

"Who do you work for?"

"I can't tell you that. It'd be a breech of confidence. Un-pro, y'know?"

"Then let me ask you this. Why would Manny Ortiz kid-nap—"

Eagle interjected, "Or kill."

I continued, "His own nephew?"

"Why does anyone *ever* do this kind of thing. Money, love, or revenge. It ain't love, so it must be one of the other two. Or both. Manny got cut out of the will, and now his brother has it all. Maybe he just wants his piece of the pie."

"Pie. Great idea. Does this diner have pie?"

"Best you'll ever taste."

Lunch was yummy. The diner was sweet. And the waitress was efficient.

Eagle was a new toy.

I held my hand up, palm up. "You really can't see that?"

Eagle squinted, looking at my hand. "I don't see it. No spark, remember."

Of course, there was nothing to see, but he didn't know that.

"How about this?" I asked, snapping my fingers.

He shook his head. "Nope."

"This?" I waved my arm over my head.

"No!" He was starting to sound frustrated.

"What do you need?" The server appeared, probably because of the wave.

I figured why waste her trip. "Could I get a piece of strawberry-rhubarb with a scoop of vanilla ice cream, please?"

"Sure, honey. And you?"

Eagle shook his head. "Nothing else for me. I'll take the check."

Once the server had gone, I rubbed my hands together then entwined the fingers inside-out and made a steeple. Here's the church. Here's the steeple. I turned them over and wiggled my fingers. Open the doors and see all the people. "Still nothing?" I asked.

He stared at my hands, then said, "Are you messing with me?"

I laughed out loud. Loudly. Spontaneously. Eagle was turning out to be a hoot.

"Here's what I don't understand," I said, cutting the last bite of pie in half to make it last longer. "Must be tough being a P.I. in Wyrdwood.”

"Because I’m normal?”

"Duh.”

"I had a sidekick for years. He was some kind of lizard kin. I never understood any of it, but he could see in the dark, run like the dickens, and sniff out a dead body at fifty yards.”

"What happened to him?”

"He’s gone.”

"Oh, I’m so sorry. How did he die?”

"No, I mean he left. Some bullshit about finding his soulmate. Whatever.”

I wanted to reach out and pat his arm, but I restrained myself. "You’ll find someone,” I said.

"I don’t need a soulmate.”

"Um, I meant a sidekick.” I then realized he may be considering me for the role—of sidekick, not soulmate. I added, "Someone not me. I have no desire to be your sidekick.”

"You?” He waved me off. "No. This job is too demanding.”

And there it was. I’d been challenged. Crap.

"I can do demanding,” I said. "I won the state championship in hundred-meter hurdles when I was in high school.”

He opened his mouth, and I knew he was going to ask how long ago that was, so I raised an index finger to halt him. "Careful,” I warned.

"How about tonight?”

I blinked at him. "What?” Immediately, the idea of a date with him bloomed in my mind, all the way from dinner to drinks to going the distance at his place.

"Tonight, I’m doing surveillance on Manny Ortiz. Come with. You can get a taste of what it’s like.”

Not a date. Okay. I wanted to breathe a sigh of relief but found myself a touch disappointed. I thought of Mom. She didn’t want me to come over, and if I went home, I’d just fret.

"Sure, why not?" I said. "I got nothing better to do. When?"

"Four-thirty? We'll go examine that lawn first. Ortiz gets off work around six most days, so we'll just roll right into it. I want to see where he goes and what he does. If he has the kid, then he just might give away the location. So, you in?"

"Just one night. Yeah. Let's do it. But we'll need snacks and sodas."

Eagle nodded, expression serious. "And sandwiches."

"You like roast beef?"

"My favorite. With spicy mustard."

"And horseradish." *Yeah,* I thought. *This could be fun.* "You should get them from Butchie's. They've got the best roast beef in town."

"I know," he said, raising a hand to catch the waitress's attention.

"You make good money doing this?"

"I do all right." He smiled, and by "all right," he meant "cha-ching!"

◆◆◆

◆

Greetings, fellow earthling.
I come in peace.

—T-shirt

◆

31

KITTY
Must wait for the money.

I relayed the kidnapper's message, and the Ortizes took the news better than I expected.

"How do you want to handle this?" I asked.

"Well," said Gregorio as he met Badahlia's gaze. "We do what they tell us to do." They both looked at me. "You're going to deliver the money." He wasn't asking, he was telling.

I was in no position to argue with him, but I was already making my own plans. In order to get that reward, I needed to reveal the kidnapper. Simply arranging for the boy's return wasn't going to be enough. And my window of opportunity was closing quickly.

"I'll do it," I said. "Can you give me your phone numbers, so I can call you when it's done?"

They each recited their numbers for me.

"What about Manny?" I asked. "Are you going to tell him about all this?"

"What for?" Gregorio asked, sounding suspicious.

"He's family, and I know he's worried about Anthony. I can fill him in, if you want. It's no trouble." What I really wanted was to confront Manny about Val's video, and I had no way to contact him.

"I think," said Badahlia, "the fewer people involved, the better. Less chance for complications."

If I argued with her, I'd look suspicious, so I didn't push it.

"Go back to the Garrett's," said Gregorio. "As soon as I

have the money, I'll bring it to you. It'll be a couple hours before it's ready."

Gregorio left to go to the bank to wait for the money. Badahlia went to prepare for her son's return—presumably to the B&B.

I followed them out then pretended to need the bathroom. The Women's was just down the hall from the elevators. I went in, held the door open a crack, and watched them get into the elevator.

Someone jerked the door from my hands, trying to get in, and startled me.

"Oh!" I said. "Excuse me. I was just...leaving."

The stranger held the door for me as I emerged and only returned my smile at the last second.

I wanted to see Janette again. She hadn't finished packing yet and was at her computer, clicking away at the keys. I stepped into the doorway to her cubicle.

"Sabotaging the company before security comes to escort you out?" I asked. I was joking.

The slyness in her smile told me I'd hit the nail on the head. Either that, or she was joking too.

"I don't have much time," she said. "H.R. has been circling. What can I do for you?"

"I came by to let you know that Badahlia has left the building."

"Awesome! That means I won't have to slink out the back."

"And, I wanted to see if you know where Manny Ortiz lives or works?"

"Yeah." She waved a hand toward the south. "He's the tapas chef at the Icarus Gallery down on Main."

"Great, thanks." I stretched one foot toward the exit.

"You know, I almost dated him instead of Gregorio."

"No kidding?"

She had nostalgia—and maybe regret—written all over

her. "He asked me out. Nothing had happened with Gregorio yet, although we were flirting a lot. Manny was…sweet and sexy. He was weird, in a good way. But Gregorio was…"

Rich?

"Safe." Janette shrugged. "Or so I thought."

"A married man is safe?" I did my best to keep judgment out of my voice.

"Sure. I figured we'd have a little fun, then he'd move on. I didn't expect to fall in love with him. Hell, I sure didn't expect *him* to fall in love with me."

"So you told Manny no?"

"Yeah."

"How'd he take it?"

Janette stretched wide her French-manicured fingers. "He just walked away. He never said another word to me. Whenever we cross paths, it's as if I'm invisible. He doesn't even acknowledge my existence."

"Did he know you were seeing Gregorio?"

"Not right away, but a few months later, he saw us together. Gregorio said they fought about it. Manny's jealous of Gregorio because Gregorio got all the brains, the looks, and…"

The money?

"Me."

"I see. Well, I better go. I want to catch him before he leaves work. Thanks for the info."

She had already turned back to her computer and was mouse-clicking.

The Icarus was a small but elite art-gallery-slash-tapas-bar that exhibited the work of Wyrdwood's artists. At any one time, it had displays by two or three locals as well as a room dedicated to artwork by the more famous of Wyrd-wood's talents. A mix of kith and Normal, the artistes worked in every medium imaginable from oils to textiles to bio to trash. Nothing was too taboo or too kitsch.

It had been years since I'd last stepped foot in the gallery. Bob had hated the pretension of it all. He was a simple man who had no patience for metaphors. He used to say, "If it's worth saying, then just say it straight."

If we went out, it was usually to an action movie. He could sit still through those, and he didn't torture me with snide commentary while I was trying to enjoy myself. I could have gone alone to the gallery, but to be honest, I didn't care that much. Art is interesting when I'm faced with it, but it was rarely an experience I sought out. My tiny artistic talent had been eviscerated in kindergarten when the other kids had mocked me for coloring outside the lines.

Weaving my way through an animatronic exhibit of strange neon sea creatures with eyes that followed me, I wondered if Pam Garrett had ever displayed her work there. I eased my way around a hot pink sea anemone with a gaping yoni-like mouth and grasping tentacles that sucked on my clothes until I pulled them away. I was pondering the metaphor when I spotted Manny in the next room.

Manny wore a black turtleneck with tailored pants and had a white apron slung over his arm. I caught myself thinking he'd grown into a fine-looking young man then remembered he might be a kidnapper. Looks, as most women know, can be deceiving.

I'd have gone straight to him, but Manny was talking to someone with animated gestures. They were arguing. I hid behind a six-foot raccoon carved out of wood and attempted to eavesdrop. I still couldn't hear them, so I went from artwork to artwork, pretending to be fascinated by the works and hiding behind them once I'd arrived. I peered out, watching the two men. The closer I got, the better I could hear.

The strange man said, "What am I s'posed to do? Huh?"

"I don't know, but I can't change my situation." Manny

began to pace a few steps back and forth, agitated. Every time he turned around to come toward me, I ducked back into hiding.

"I've got clients lined up, Manny. You can't just leave 'em hanging. It's gonna look bad."

"I get it! Tell them it's my fault. I'm doing the best I can, but I just don't have it right now."

"Well, you better get it, 'cause if you don't, all hell's gonna break loose, and it ain't gonna end well for you. All it takes is one word. One word in the wrong ear and you're dead forever. Remember that."

"Yeah, yeah." Manny stopped pacing and took several steps away from the other man. "I need to get back to work. I'll call you. Soon as I have an update."

The man walked by me and caught me watching him.

"What're *you* lookin' at?" he demanded though he didn't stop walking.

I shook my head and pretended to scrutinize the painting of a green apple. Just a green apple on a black background, floating in empty space like a moon, like a fertile ovum, like the offer of knowledge from the tree of good and evil, like the promise of immortality through progeny. I smiled. Maybe I still had an artistic bone after all.

The man left the room. Once he had, I casually emerged from my hiding place.

Manny, however, was gone. Not just from the room, but from the gallery. By the time I got to the exit, he was getting in his car. I couldn't catch him.

The apple had made me hungry, so I decided to give myself a break and get lunch. The gallery's tapas were too expensive, so I strolled down Main Street toward the Mousehole café with my hands in my pockets and a jumble of thoughts running through my brain. Foremost among them, I wondered whether Anthony Ortiz was alive, and if so, was he comfortable?

While I was eating my egg-salad sandwich at the café, I had an idea. It hit me like a freight train. What if Val had captured the kidnapper on video the night he dropped off the ransom note? I gobbled down the rest of my sandwich on the way to the garbage can and scooted out the door. I could have called Val, but interrupting his day appealed to me.

Val was home and did answer the door, though he stood squarely on the threshold so I couldn't enter.

"What's wrong?" he asked, dropping his eyelids to half-mast.

"Nothing." I held my hands up in surrender. "Well, something, I guess. You know they still haven't found Anthony Ortiz, right?"

"Right."

"So..." I suddenly doubted whether I should tell him. I looked into his eyes. "Can I trust you?"

He blinked in surprise. "Depends," he said. "What's this about?"

"In for a penny, in for a pound," I told myself.

"What are you talking about?" Val asked.

"The kidnapper showed up at the Garrett's last night. To leave a ransom note on the front door. I didn't see who it was."

Val's eyebrows went way up. "Why are you telling me this?"

I continued, "Your security cameras?"

"Last night, you say?"

"Around two a.m."

Val put one hand high on the doorframe and leaned there. It made him seem taller. "My cameras were down. I'm getting new, higher resolution ones installed later today, so I had to take the old ones off."

"You're kidding?"

"Nope."

Indeed, the camera on the front corner was missing when I looked for it.

I wanted to accuse Val of doing that on purpose, but I had no proof. The only way he could have known that the kidnapper was going to be there was if he *was* the kidnapper.

"Okay," I said. "Never mind." Disappointed, excitement crushed, I headed toward my car.

"Hey, Kitty," he called after me.

I glanced back.

"Who knows you're catsitting at that house?"

It was a good question. "The neighbors," I replied. "Diana. The Garretts, of course. Lots of folks."

"You be careful," he said, and I believed he cared.

◆◆◆

◆

**Meet me halfway
And we can have a picnic.**

—sticker on a telephone pole

◆

32

MUSE
Loses his guard-cat license.

A man wearing an orange sheet walked up to the Garrett's front door and knocked. I was inside, watching from my perch on the back of the couch. Greta came out of her nest, looked at me, then stared at the door. She was willing the man to go away. Silly child.

The fact that he wasn't lurking but was coming into the house as bold as you please, made me think he probably belonged there. I didn't stop him. Far be it from me to interrupt potential entertainment. Besides, Kitty wasn't there, so the only person he could harm was Greta...meh.

I could have kicked him out. On principal, I didn't trust anyone without fur on their head—and he had none—but it was my naptime. I chose to take the high road. That time.

I watched him with interest as he went from room to room to confirm that no one was home. While he was upstairs, I climbed down and sniffed his basket. It smelled of grass and spices. I sneezed on it.

When he returned, he took the basket into the living room. It contained a bowl, a plate, incense, a candle, matches, a bouquet of white flowers, a cloth, and other things I didn't recognize. He poured water into the bowl, lit the candle and the incense, and spread out his cloth. He sat down on it, and then the singing began—if you can call it that. The language was foreign to me, but I could tell it just repeated ad nauseam.

At first, I rocked in time with the droning tune and learned the words by phonetics, if not by meaning. Then, the bitter stank of the incense overwhelmed me. It reminded me of the old priests from before my exile, the "wise" ones who taught us all to appreciate ritual and the power of punishment. These weren't necessarily good memories, so I shrank deeper into the shadows under the ottoman.

The chanting went on for an age, repetitive, redundant, and ridiculous. I eventually relaxed onto my side and dozed. Thus, when he suddenly got to his feet, it startled me. I was glad, however, for some movement.

He picked up the bowl and went from room to room, singing and splashing water everywhere. At one point, he even managed to get Greta. She gave an undignified yowl and scooted out of her hiding place. I have no idea where she went, but I didn't see her again all evening. If she didn't react well to holy water, did that mean my suspicion that she was a demon was justified?

The monk—I'd put two and two together—blessed the whole house. He did his due diligence even though Greta and I were the only witnesses. By the time he was done, I was starving and willing Kitty to appear.

She did. Walked right in the front door and screamed.

The monk just looked at her.

I flicked my tail and walked over to rub her ankles.

◆◆◆

33

KITTY
Is punked by a monk.

It wasn't my fault. The Buddhist monk had not called in advance to warn me he'd be there. When I walked in and saw a strange man, I screamed. As soon as my brain registered his bald head and off-the-shoulder robe, I put a hand to my heart and bowed my head. Not in reverence, but because I was having a heart attack.

"Sorry!" I said. "You scared me."

The monk barely moved. He said, "Know from the rivers in clefts and crevices, those in small channels flow noisily. The great flow is silent. Whatever's not full makes noise."

"Um, okay," I replied. "Thank you?"

He looked long and hard at my face then stepped toward me. I nearly retreated, but thought it might be considered rude.

I met his gaze, head partially turned to the side.

The chanting started low, a rumble in his chest. It grew in speed and volume, an uninterrupted refrain of rhythmic words.

He took the bamboo brush and swished it in the water bowl, then he flicked water directly into my face.

"Oh!" I cried out. I dropped my chin to dodge some of the splash.

He chanted and splashed, sang and flicked. It went on so long I had time to wonder whether he was blessing me, exorcising the evil inside me, or hosting a wet t-shirt contest.

I couldn't move my feet.

As an afterthought, I folded my hands in front of my chest—the generic prayer posture. I hoped it conveyed respect. I prayed the assault would stop.

The monk broke his chant to say, "An insincere and evil friend is more to be feared than a wild beast. A wild beast may wound your body, but an evil friend will wound your mind. Ardently do today what must be done. Who knows? Tomorrow, death comes."

I blinked several times.

With a nod, the monk walked into the living room, his sandals shuffling on the hardwood. He stood over a small wicker picnic basket and put his tools into it, giving each one the extra attention of a blessing. At the end, he had only the half-filled bowl, which he carried to me.

"For Pamela," he said. "Do not discard it. She will know what to do."

I took it genteelly from him. "If I can ask," I said, "what exactly do you mean by 'Tomorrow, death comes'?"

The monk patted me on the shoulder. "If *you* knew what I know about the power of giving, you would not let a single meal pass without sharing it in some way."

Holding the bowl in both hands, I followed him back to the basket.

"But..." I said, confused. "What?"

"Death is not to be feared by one who his lived wisely. No one saves us but ourselves. No one can, and no one may. You yourself must walk the path. Strive on diligently. Don't give up."

I held the bowl against the middle of my chest and asked, "Do you know something I don't?" I felt my eyebrows meet in the middle and actively relaxed them. "I mean... I'm caught in a dangerous situation right now. You know?"

The monk's eyes were dark and deep, but I saw a twinkle in them that unnerved me. He had a spark. That meant he might *actually* know something about my future. He said,

"Nothing is forever except change."

Unsatisfied by that answer, I followed him to the door and out onto the porch. At the bottom of the porch stairs, he turned back and said, "Do not spill a drop. It must go to Pamela."

I looked down into the bowl and saw my own reflection there. I'd gotten so old. My double chin and baggy eyes, my saggy jowls and thinning lips all stared back at me—metaphorically speaking. When I lifted my head again, the monk was gone.

I figured he'd disappeared, teleported into a pocket realm, or flown away—until I saw him drive by in an old gray Chevy sedan. It sputtered and backfired but kept going.

He turned the corner at the end of the block and chugged out of sight.

I went back inside and set the water bowl on the dining table.

That was when I noticed that the pie was gone. It wasn't where I'd left it, and it wasn't anywhere I searched either. The monk had stolen the last of my pie. The last of *my* pie. I'd been looking forward to that pie, especially knowing that it might be my last meal.

"Poop," I said aloud.

Muse, the cat, came down off the back of the couch and stretched up my leg. I sat down and welcomed him into my lap.

"That guy was weird," I said. "Right?"

The black cat gave a little hiss of agreement. It sounded almost like, "Sheesh."

I stroked his lush fur.

♦♦♦

◆

**A purr a day
keeps the doctor away.**

—poster seen at the vet's office

◆

34

DIANA
Researches the suspects.

The Internet grabbed me by the eyeballs and wouldn't let go. After my lunch with Eagle, I'd returned to the office to continue my searches on Manny Ortiz and Val Krall. I'd started with Manny, since Eagle and I were planning on stalking him—I mean "staking him out"—that evening. What I found surprised me.

I browsed his social media sites and uncovered pictures of him with his rich and famous friends—skiing, surfing, and sunbathing, not to mention dining, drinking, and dancing. The more I looked, the more my face grew sallow and saggy. Dang. Manny wasn't just a playboy playah, he was a wealthy one.

I'd seen him behind the counter at the Icarus, ordering around his sous-chefs as if he were in Barcelona. To me, he'd always looked like an uppity fast-food worker. The only thing missing was a nametag. I'd assumed that, because he was working, his cookbook hadn't done so well. Wow, was I wrong.

At Icarus, he made daily videos related to the tapas he was inventing, cooking, and serving. He posted these on the web, and—to my shock—they catered to over half a million subscribers. He went by Chef Emmanuel and posted a new tapas recipe every day. I watched several of his videos, and even though I'd just had lunch, he made my mouth water.

The videos promoted the gallery, but more than that, they promoted his cookbook. And, he was about to release a second one. Manny wasn't only rich, he was famous.

So, of course, I had to look into his relationship status next. As far as I could tell, he wasn't dating anyone specific. Okay.

I stored all that information away then turned my browser toward Valentine Krall—specifically to finding out whether he had a son. This proved more difficult, since Val had no online presence that I could find. The guy was off the grid.

The only reference I found was a decades-old article in Architect Archive, a trade magazine long extinct. He had a brief mention as one of the architects who designed the Highlight apartment complex. The article mentioned Val's father, Earl S. Krall, also an architect, who worked at the same firm. That led me to searching the obituaries. Earl had merited a small mention in the Wyrdwood Gazette when he died, and it said he was "survived by his son Valentine (Martha) Krall and grandson Robert Krall."

There it was. I whooped aloud, causing several people in the office to turn and stare at me.

"Sorry. Big sale at the computer store," I told them, and they lost interest. I screen-captured the obituary.

Martha Krall, Val's wife or ex-wife, was even more elusive than Val himself. Robert Krall, on the other hand, was all over the internet. He was twenty-eight and living in Seattle. He worked for the park district as a landscaper. I stopped there. He obviously had no involvement in Anthony's kidnapping.

Then, feeling quite full of myself, I did a search on Eagle Crenshaw. I found his business website, Eagle-Eye Investigations. Cute name. The site was succinct and factual. His bio mentioned his military history, his Bachelor's in criminal psychology, and his black belt in Karate. There was a photo of him there, in a corn field, staring off into the distance with a camera in his hand. The trees behind him had no leaves, so it was winter, and he had a heroic quality about him. I studied that image longer than I should have.

My computer chimed to let me know it was four p.m., and so I started shutting down. I wanted to be outside, waiting, when Eagle came to get me.

◆◆◆

◆

**Don't mind me.
I'm just a little old lady
detective who knows all your secrets
and will find all the bodies.**

—falsely attributed to Miss Marple

◆

35

MUSE
Spies trouble.

Kitty let me out to make my rounds. I had to check on my growing pile of treasures. Little Manny Man's frantic search of the lawn made me purr. He came like a thief in the night, when no one would see him. Silly human. He had squirreled away so many trinkets, burying them in the lawn. It made no sense to me. Why not just take them away? Why bury them in their little plastic baggies? Why mark them with golf tees? He'd obviously intended to dig them back up, but it seemed like way too much trouble. I've known people who like to torture themselves. I hadn't thought Manny was one of those.

The burying was a complex Easter egg hunt. Was it, however, for himself or for someone else? Had the joker buried the treasure so he could entertain the nobility? Hm. He certainly had entertained the king.

I hoped he'd show up again that evening.

As the sun slid toward the horizon, I waited on the porch of Greta's house, near my Kitty. She was in danger. I felt it in my tail fur. I was ready to defend her if so required. With each passing meal, I grew more fond of her.

My haunches suddenly itched for movement and launched me out of my seat and onto the grass. I sprinted around the corner of the house, my back claws digging into the dirt. I ran and took great joy in the running. My body felt strong and agile, quick and responsive. I pushed myself to the limit then stopped just as abruptly as I'd started. I foomphed onto one side in the grass to catch my breath.

Such a glorious day! The sun was aglow with orange light as it hovered just above nightfall. I was alive. I was free. And my belly was full. Life was good.

I sat up, lifted my back leg, bent to give my undercarriage a lick, and came face to face with a pair of eyes. They were on the other side of the dirty basement window, staring out at me. I leapt back onto my feet, ready for a fight. My back went up. My fur went up, and a hiss emerged from me without my bidding. My instincts have always been keen.

The eyes disappeared.

Erring on the side of caution, unwilling to be an easy target for any predator, I ran back to the front of the house and yowled to be let in. I had to protect Kitty too.

◆◆◆

36

KITTY
Receives the ransom money.

Muse was making a racket on the front porch. With more than a little trepidation, I peeked out to see what was happening. My first thought was that the kidnapper had arrived before the money did, but all I found was Muse sitting expectantly on the welcome mat, mrowling.

I opened the door. "You want to come in, kitten?"

His answer was to zoom in. He made a beeline for the kitchen and sat staring at the basement door, tail twitching.

I returned to fretting about the ransom money. It had been over two hours since I'd left the Badahlia's office building, and I hadn't heard from Gregorio. I considered calling him a hundred times and even pulled up his contact information more than once. I refrained, however. He couldn't rush the bank any more than I could hurry him.

The sun went down, and so I made a trip around the house turning on lights. I also double-checked the locks on all the doors and windows.

I thought about Anthony. Poor kid. I tortured myself imagining his little chubby face gone pale as a ghost, his eyes huge and wet with so many tears, and his chin trembling. I imagined him curling up into a ball to make himself as small as possible. Envisioning it brought tears to my own eyes.

I had to save him. I was determined to do whatever it took to get him back—even if I didn't get the reward. In many ways, I had his life in my hands. That outweighed my financial troubles.

The waiting was difficult. I thought about the ransom delivery.

What would I need? I had my most comfortable walking shoes on. I might need a sweater. Should I take a weapon? A kitchen knife maybe? A box cutter? Did Pamela even have a box cutter? I wasted time searching through drawers looking for one before giving up. Knowing me, I'd probably have cut myself anyway.

I did find some protein bars and put one in my pocket. Who knew how long I'd be out there running from phone booth to phone booth. I was thirsty, but I didn't want to have to look for a powder room while delivering the ransom. I picked up a notepad and pen, realizing that I was unlikely to remember any instructions they gave me for longer than thirty seconds. I found a bandana and tied it on my head like a sweatband. What else? What else? I wanted to be ready for any contingency.

Greta followed me from room to room, pausing only to hiss at Muse when she passed him. When I sat down on the couch to wait, she stalked around me, gradually getting closer, until finally she sat down beside my thigh and curled up to nap. I petted her head, and she didn't complain.

"Sweet girl," I whispered. "I'm so glad we can be friends." I closed my eyes and focused on the softness of her fur.

When the doorbell rang, I nearly leapt out of my skin, and Greta launched herself off the couch.

It took me longer to get up, but then I snuck to the window and looked out.

Gregorio stood on the porch with a large briefcase clutched to his chest.

When I opened the door, he said, "I hate this."

I understood. "Do you want to come in?"

He shook his head and thrust the briefcase at me. "Better not. They might be watching."

I hugged the briefcase to my chest and glanced up and down the street. "You think?"

"I would."

"Okay." My heart beat a little faster even though I didn't see any unfamiliar cars.

"Do exactly what they say."

"I'll do my best."

"Do it right, Kitty. My son's life depends on it."

All I could do was nod.

"Call me as soon as it's done."

"I will."

"The *minute* it's done."

"Okay. I promise."

Gregorio hovered on the doorstep until, finally, he said, "Good luck," then turned and walked back to his car.

I shut the door and stood with my back to it, looking at Pamela's foyer, living room, and dining room. I was holding five-hundred-thousand dollars in my arms, a half a million. The thought alone caused my legs to freeze.

Muse jumped onto the dining table. He seemed tense and alert.

"What do you think, Muse? I should put this somewhere out of sight, right?"

The cat paced.

"Maybe I should check it first? Make sure it's all there?" I shifted my weight from foot to foot to get the feeling back. "I mean, what if Gregorio is putting one over on me? It could get me killed. I should take a look. Real quick." I moved to the dining table and set the briefcase down beside Muse.

The locks were standard and, with two sharp clicks, I released the lid. I opened it a crack, got sight of the neat stacks of one-hundred-dollar bills, and froze again. "Damn," I said. "I could pay off my mortgage with this." It was more money than I'd seen in my entire life. Would they miss it if I took a single packet of bills? Or two? Didn't I deserve a little recompense for putting myself in danger?

A little voice in my head said, "No one will notice." I liked that voice a lot.

Then, however, a different voice—my mother's voice—said, "The kidnappers will notice."

I sighed.

Muse was trying to squeeze into the briefcase, sniffing at the cash. I had to push his head out in order to close it.

The sound of the locks re-latching made me relax a bit. I looked around to find a place to stash the case and decided to hide it behind a leather recliner. It was close enough that I could grab it if I had to leave in a hurry but hidden enough that even the Buddhist monk wouldn't have noticed it.

I thought again of my stolen pie and cursed the monk. That led me to think about cat food. I decided to feed Greta and Muse early, so they'd have it if the kidnappers called and I had to scoot. As I was pouring out an overabundance of kibble, my phone buzzed. I glanced over at the display.

Aloud, I hissed, "Shazbot! It's Pamela. I don't want to talk to her." How could I tell her that a kidnapper had come to her door? I didn't want to lie to her, and I didn't want her to interfere. She'd have gone straight to the police if I told her. Besides, what if the kidnappers tried to contact me while I was talking to her?

I didn't answer.

The call reminded me, however, to text Diana. I thumbed, "Got the money. Waiting. All good." Concise. Direct. It was one of those situations. I waited a minute, but all I got back was a tiny smile emoji. It was unsatisfying.

◆◆◆

37

DIANA
Rides with Eagle.

Eagle was on time. I respected that. I'm a bit obsessive about being on time—or early—myself. I find it's far easier to be early and have to wait than it is to be late and have to run. I don't like running.

I dropped into his passenger seat and shut the door. I took the time to put on my seatbelt before speaking a single word. Finally, I half-turned toward him and asked, "Okay, how does this work?"

Eagle was watching me. Half-turned toward me, he answered, "Pretty soon, Manny will be leaving work. We follow him."

"No problem," I said. "I'm ready. Let's go."

He didn't reply but turned back to the front and put the car in gear.

I found it easy to be silent with Eagle. Maybe it was because there was so much going on beneath the surface and so much adventure on the horizon too. I didn't need to fill the void because there wasn't one. He and I were living larger than life. In any minute, the world could turn upside down, or we could catch a serial killer.

My phone chimed. "Sorry," I said, playing my role. "I have to take this." I pulled the phone from my pocket and looked at it. It was Mom. She'd texted me. "Got teh mony. Waitinng. All goof"

It took me two read-throughs to figure out what she meant. I sent her an ironic smiley in return. Glancing sideways at Eagle, I wondered whether I should tell him about the kidnapping, the ransom, and the fact that my mom was the sacrificial lamb. I decided against it. For one thing, Mom would have killed me. For another, I had no guarantee he wouldn't try to be the hero and get Mom killed.

I was worried about her, but I knew better than to try to save her. She wouldn't thank me for it. She was tough, and if she needed help, she'd call. I could still hear her saying, "Stay in your own lane," whenever my dad had tried to rescue her. I've seen her fix dishwashers, install new electrical outlets, and out-drive the craziest mothers in the drop-off line. She'd spent her whole adult life as a mom and a housewife, and it had given her mad skills. It had also made her fearless. She'd always said that her job was to wrestle bears, and by that, she meant parent-teacher conferences, recital costumes, and a houseful of teenage girls. Why she couldn't have taken more of an interest in the household budget, I didn't understand. Division of labor, I suppose.

No, Mom would be okay. I had to believe that. Besides, I was still convinced that the kidnapper was one of the Ortizes, thus not terribly dangerous at all.

"So." I watched the scenery slide by. "You think Manny is the kidnapper?"

"Dunno. All I know is that he's one sketchy dude."

"What about Gregorio? He's got motive. His wife's about to take half his assets."

Eagle stole a glance at me. "Nah. I know Gregorio didn't do it."

"Really? How?"

"I had eyes on him when it happened."

"So that was you!"

"What was me?" Eagle swerved to miss a pothole.

I bumped against the door and grabbed the oh-shit bar. "The spooky mofo in the photo, watching Gregorio outside his girlfriend's place. The cops have you on video, but it was impossible to tell it was you."

"They know I was there?"

"No. That's what I said. They couldn't make you out. The image wasn't clear enough."

"Good."

"Why were you tailing Gregorio?"

"Detective-client privilege," Eagle replied. "I can't tell you the details."

"But we're practically partners. You can tell me."

When Eagle kept silent, I decided to push him. "Let me guess. Someone hired you to find out if Gregorio was having an affair. Someone, maybe, whose name begins with a B?"

The hesitation was ripe, but Eagle eventually said, "Maybe."

In my head, I was celebrating.

Then, he said, "Maybe not."

"Oh, come on!" I protested. "It's obvious. Badahlia hired you to find out if he's cheating on her."

"She already knew. She needed proof."

"Aha!" I pumped a fist in the air. Then, I thought it through. "Wait. She knew?"

"That's what I said. She had a plan to ensure a good outcome from the divorce. I was gathering evidence."

"I get it now. She was going to take a big bite out of the Ortiz inheritance. We've eliminated Gregorio. And Badahlia was getting drunk in the bar. Therefore...if the inheritance is the motive, then it must be Manny. However, Manny wouldn't inherit it anyway. It would all go to Anthony. Which means, if it's Manny, then maybe he doesn't plan to return Anthony alive. Then, he'd be one step closer to all that money." I sat up a little straighter. "Maybe the fire was meant to kill Anthony!"

Eagle snorted out his nose, the equivalent of a small laugh. He said, "Well, it's either Manny or some rando off the street. It's possible the kid was just in the wrong place at the wrong time."

I found that difficult to accept and said, "I don't think this was random. Whoever the kidnapper is, they seem to know a lot about the Ortizes and the neighborhood. Heck, it could even be you, for all I know."

Eagle pulled up to the curb in front of the Icarus Gallery. He reached over me, tugged the door handle, and pushed the door open. "Hop out," he said. "They've got an order of appetizers for us at the gallery. It's to-go, and it's already paid for. See if you spot Manny. If he leaves, come straight back here."

"You're kidding."

"Nope."

"What're *you* gonna do?"

"I'm going to stay here so we don't lose him if he bounces while you're in there."

I undid my seatbelt and got out of the car. "The order is under your name?"

"Emmanuel Rodriguez."

"One of your aliases?"

"Just go. It's almost quitting time."

"Okay, okay." I shut the car door and scuttled down the sidewalk to the gallery. Before I got there, the enticing rifts of a Spanish guitar drifted out. Once inside, I inhaled the many aromas of the tapas and the people who ate them. The gallery wasn't so busy as the restaurant. It was almost dinner time, after all. Happy hour to some. My stomach growled.

I got in line at the counter and scanned around, looking for Manny. He was nowhere in sight. Before long, it was my turn. I stepped up and said "Hi" to a tall, skinny, high-school-age teen working his first job and plainly bored as a fence.

"Welcome to the Icarus." He didn't bother to look me in the eye. "What can I get you?"

"I have a to-go order under Rodriguez," I said.

The teen moved down the counter to search through an array of bags waiting there.

I followed him. "You like working with Manny Ortiz?" I asked.

"What?"

"Just curious. Is he nice?"

"I don't know." He picked through the to-go bags, looking for mine. I saw the one labeled 'Rodriguez' just beyond where the guy was searching.

"He in the kitchen?"

"What?"

"Ya know. Ortiz. Is he in the kitchen?"

"No. He left early today."

I gasped. "You're kidding!"

"No. Why would I?"

I scooted over to where my bag was and held it up to him. "Here it is. Thanks!" I left the kid staring after me as I speed-walked back to Eagle's car.

◆◆◆

◆

**I believe in magick.
I believe in you.**

—lyrics from "You Spark Me" by Anpu

◆

38

MUSE
Solves a mystery.

I could have sharpened my claws on the tension in that house. The later the hour, the more anxious the Kitty. The box she'd hidden behind the soft chair had a stench like Papa Ortiz. The paper inside it smelled like greed. Whoever had that annoying boy-child was asking for money in exchange for his life. Personally, if it were up to me, I'd have rejected the offer. Anthony wasn't worth that much.

Me, I was focused on the basement door. Someone was down there. I hadn't recognized who in the gloom of twilight and through the dust on the window. However, I knew predatory eyes when I saw them.

I tried to draw Kitty's attention to the basement door. I howled in front of it, and she thought I was hungry. I scratched it, and she yelled at me. I horked up a hairball—not easy to do on command—and she just cleaned it up.

Finally, I meowed at the front door, and she let me out. What choice did I have but to give up? Humans could be so thick sometimes. I wanted desperately to communicate with her. That was not, however, a skill in my magickal toolbox. If it was in hers, then she had yet to take it out and swing it around.

I paused to sharpen my claws on the trunk of the maple tree. I needed a plan. On reflection, there was only one thing to be done. I had to go into the basement and somehow make enough noise to get Kitty's attention.

Night had fallen hard, and the moon was a distant glow

behind clouds. I didn't mind. I blended into the darkness, kept close to the house, and crept—belly to grass—toward the window where I'd seen the eyes.

They weren't there anymore, but a mysterious light tinted the glass.

I had to get inside. On the back of the house, a different window had long since come unlatched. No one had noticed because it was behind a curtain. I'd spent many nights sleeping in the warmth and quiet of the Garrett basement whenever the Ortizes had tossed me out.

With a hop, I rushed past the window and made my way around to the back. The other window was ajar.

My senses grew even sharper as I approached, sniffing, listening, and scanning. I sensed the Ortizes. Whoever was in there was an Ortiz. That made my hackles rise. The members of that family were ruthless, and I could easily imagine any one of them breaking my neck. It was a testimony to my prowess that I'd survived living with them for as long as I had.

Bravely, I pulled the window outward. It swung on hinges at the top, and with a poke of my nose, I squeezed through. I tried—and failed—to be quick so it wouldn't shut on my tail. Normally, I'm quite agile, but the frame came down on the very tip. It hurt worse than a scratch to the nose. I wanted to yowl, but I contained it, turning it into a low growl instead. I hunkered down and waited for the throb to stop.

As far as I could tell, the predator remained unaware of my presence, and I relaxed. The interior stunk even stronger of Ortiz. I listened, switching my ears this way and that to catch any sound. I heard breathing and the shuffle of fabric. The smack of a mouth, eating, and the crunch of bones, breaking, made me hungry again. What was it eating? Was it a mouse? A bird? A baby rabbit?

I stuck my head out to see, leaning forward.

The surface under me tilted abruptly, and I was thrown

off-balance. Not to worry, I always—almost—land on my feet. I did not appreciate, however, having my presence revealed.

I heard a gasp before I hit the floor and took off running to find a new hiding place. My claws found no purchase on the concrete floor, and I slipped and scrabbled in my panic.

The Ortiz pursued!

Every moment counted. Every turn to throw the Ortiz off my tail was critical to my survival. I ducked under a shelf unit and forged a path through cobwebs in an effort to avoid death. I tried to climb higher, to get myself out of reach, but the fabric slipped downward and dropped me back into the Ortiz's clutches. Even as I felt hands grabbing for me, I hissed and clawed, and scrambled away from sure doom.

By pure ingenuity, I found a dark corner behind a pile of junk and eluded my pursuer. I was out of reach but did not relax. The Ortiz and I had made quite a racket, and I was hopeful that Kitty had heard. I listened intently, for I could not see the Ortiz.

Would she call the police?

Would they bring handcuffs?

Would the Ortiz flee?

Would there be a brawl?

A gun fight?

Would the Ortiz hurt Kitty?

I dropped low and made myself silent. The Ortiz did the same. Together, we listened for the crossing of footsteps on the floor above, for the door knob, the squeak of hinges, and the tentative query cast down the stairs, "Hello?"

We heard none of that. Kitty wasn't coming. My own sense of relief surprised me. I did not want Kitty to die.

Suddenly, a face appeared in the space in front of me. It startled a hiss and a growl out of me, and my body lurched upward all by itself. My hair stood on end. My claws came to ready. I bared my teeth...

And then my mind caught up with the rest of me.

That dirty, rotten scoundrel's breath blew foul across my nose, and I recoiled. The fog of his odorous body rolled in, and I hissed again.

When he reached his grubby hand through the junk to grab me, I fought a surge of panic and lashed out.

He pulled back and spewed curses at me. The scratch was already bleeding.

I renewed my commitment to hating him. My heart slowed back down and my fur settled.

The Ortiz wouldn't make that mistake again.

With rich satisfaction, I opened my mouth and yowled at the top of my lungs.

"Shut up!" the Ortiz hissed, along with more expletives.

I narrowed my eyes at him and did it again—and then again. On the third one, the sound of Kitty's footsteps sounded overhead, moving toward the basement door. I put my heart, soul, and hatred into the next yowl. My opinion had changed. Kitty needed to see this.

◆◆◆

39

KITTY
Descends into the Underworld.

The kidnappers called. My hand shook as I answered.
"Hello?"
"You the catsitter?"
"Yeah, it's me. You the kidnapper?"
"Shut up. I need you to be ready to go at dawn. I'll call again then. Get some sleep, you're going to need it." They hung up before I could say anything else.

After that, I'd put my phone on the charger for a while and killed time by petting Greta, cleaning the litter box, and making myself some tea. By nine, I couldn't stop yawning. It had been a long day.

I decided to take the kidnapper's advice and lie down, but not before I set three alarms and positioned my phone next to the bed so I'd hear when they called.

I was asleep before my head hit the pillow.

Then, Muse started caterwauling. The clock said it was almost ten o'clock. I'd been asleep for less than an hour. I crawled out of bed and stumbled back down to the living room, toward the sound of his voice. He didn't sound like he wanted in. He sounded like he was being tortured. I took Pamela's statue with me again, for defense, just in case.

I couldn't tell where he was, at first, but as I searched for him, I realized that he must have gotten into the basement.

The door to the basement was in the kitchen.

I hesitated with my hand on the knob. My instincts were

telling me to proceed with caution. Or maybe not to proceed at all.

When Muse cried out again, I had no doubt something was wrong. I turned the knob and opened the door. A rectangle of light spilled down the stairs ahead of me.

"Hello?" I called. "Muse?" I waited a beat.

Muse gave another plaintive mrowr.

"Come here, kitty. You're okay." I stepped onto the top stair and bent to peer into the darkness. I could only see vague outlines. "Here, kitty kitty kitty. Come to me."

I searched for, found, and flipped on the light switch at the top of the stairs. It made a satisfying click, and light filled the basement. I headed down, being careful on the unfamiliar steps.

"Muse? Where are you, baby?"

The Garretts used their basement for storage. A pile of boxes tilted to one side against the wall, and metal shelves held plastic bins in varying sizes and colors. A large cardboard box labeled "Christmas Tree" stood in a corner, and on the far side, a pile of old garden tools and accessories lay in disarray.

To my left, just past the staircase, someone had pushed aside the chaos of the basement. Not neatly, but with a definite purpose, they'd created a clearing that made no sense to me. As I looked at it, trying to understand what I was seeing, I realized someone had been living there. An air mattress had blankets and pillows piled on it. Dirty dishes lay strewn around the area. I saw a half-eaten loaf of bread and an open jam jar with a spoon stuck in it. And, as if it were a centerpiece, my pie plate sat in the middle of it all. Empty—licked clean even—it taunted me.

All I could think was that the monk hadn't stolen it after all.

But who?

A scuffling sound drew my attention, and I crept up on

it, afraid of what I'd find.

"Muse? Is that you, honey?"

I followed the sound to a hiding spot behind some metal shelves and stuck my head carefully around the corner.

There, I discovered Anthony Ortiz, looking back at me with a blank expression. He was dressed in dirty pajamas and a hoodie. His suede slippers were darkened with mud. He didn't look any worse for wear, although he needed a shower and a toothbrush.

"Anthony!" I cried and rushed forward, squeezing in between the shelf unit and the wall to take him in my arms.

He cringed away from me, pushing hard against my breasts with his little hands, so I let him go. I had to wiggle my way back out of the space. I nearly toppled the shelves.

"Are you okay? Have you been here the whole time? What's going on?" My confusion made my voice high-pitched and strange to my ears. "How did you get in here?"

Anthony just stared at me like a deer caught in the headlights.

"But wait," I said, trying to reconcile the fact that Anthony was there with the fact that I hadn't paid the ransom yet. "Did you escape?"

"Are you going to call my parents?" Anthony lifted his chin as if challenging me.

"Of course!" I replied. "Don't worry. I'll call right now. They miss—"

The beefy eight-year-old opened his mouth and let out a scream that made me put my hands over my ears.

◆◆◆

◆

Well, shiver me whiskers.

—Muse, *King of Cats in Exile*

◆

40

DIANA
Tracks down Manny.

Eagle and I drove around, searching for Manny. We went by the Ortiz house, hit a couple places where Eagle said Manny hung out, and even spent some time watching Manny's girlfriend's house. The fact that Manny had a girlfriend was news to me.

Manny was nowhere to be found, so we parked outside his apartment building in the hope he'd show. By the time we gave up, we'd eaten all the tapas from the gallery.

"Well, hell," said Eagle. "We lost him."

"Technically," I replied, "He lost us. So, what do we do now?"

"It's almost eight. If he comes home now, it'll be to settle in for the night. He's already done whatever kidnapper business he had to do. I guess we try again tomorrow. I'll stake him out while he's at work, so we don't miss him again."

I thought about Mom and the ransom delivery. It seemed obvious to me that Manny was tied up with all that. Where else would he be? Mom hadn't texted me again, so either she was in the thick of it, or the kidnapper hadn't contacted her. I stayed on the look-out as Eagle pulled away from the curb in front of Manny's building.

Should I tell Eagle about the ransom?

Should we go stake-out the Garrett place?

I had mixed feelings about it, and maybe Eagle would know what to do. If we went to the Garrett's, and the kidnapper spotted us, they might think they'd been betrayed.

It might scuttle the entire operation, and all we'd have left would be a dead kid. Ooh, dark. No, we couldn't do that.

"Let's just drive around and see if we can spot his car," I suggested. "We can start at the gallery and work our way outward."

"Probably a waste of time." Eagle groaned.

"What have we got to lose?"

"Time. Gas. Daylight."

"Daylight's been gone for hours. Let me try this. No guarantee it will work though."

"What?"

"Hold on. Be quiet for a minute."

I held my hand up, thumb and forefinger touching to make an O. I held the "lens" to my eye and looked around. "Yeah," I said. "Head for Old Town downtown."

"You serious?"

"Dead serious." I met his gaze and lifted my eyebrows. Of course, there was no magick involved—that I knew of. I just wasn't ready to go home. I was enjoying playing detective with Eagle Rodriguez. He was easy on the eyes, and he made a perfect straight-man for my humor. Mostly, though, it was that he was easy on the eyes.

Besides, if I went home, I'd obsess on Mom and probably go down there and mess up the plan.

"Hurry," I said, "or we'll miss him."

Eagle—bless him—did exactly that. Within minutes, we were pulling onto Main Street in Old Town Wyrdwood. As a general rule, the businesses in Wyrdwood stayed open until midnight. Some even later. Because so many of the residents were nocturnal, the extended hours allowed the brick-and-mortars to attract more customers.

At night, Old Town came to life.

I watched for Manny's car while Eagle watched for jay-walking pedestrians. We'd made it almost to the southern end of Main Street when a familiar vehicle caught my eye down an alley.

"Wait!" I cried twisting around in my seat as Eagle drove on by. "Go back. I think I saw it."

After a u-turn, I showed Eagle where to stop, and we disembarked.

The alley—labeled "Danger Alley"—was one-way because it was barely wide enough to fit a single car. The vehicle I'd spotted certainly looked like Manny's. He'd parked it in the middle where he would have blocked any other traffic if there were any.

As we approached the car, I had my suspicions confirmed.

Eagle said, "Your little trick actually worked."

I laughed. "Beginner's luck," I replied, knowing full well that I had no such trick.

"Do it again, see if you can tell where he went."

That, right there, was the reason you don't fake magick. People start expecting you to use it. I made my finger circle and pretended to scan the area.

Several businesses had doors on the alley. They weren't nice glass doors with display windows beside them. They were steel security doors with peep windows through which you were vetted before being allowed inside. This usually meant they were kith-only establishments. I wasn't personally familiar with any of them, though I could just make out the sound of music and competing dialogue coming out of one of them. I wasn't worried about Eagle not getting in. They let humans in so long as they were accompanied by a magick wielder.

"I been in some of these," Eagle said. "Bar, illegal poker, excellent hobbit restaurant, and a pawn shop." He pointed at each door in turn.

"Shhh. I'm concentrating." I leaned against Manny's car and screwed up my face in concentration. Eagle bought the act—hook, line, and sinker. I reminded myself it was an adventure, did a little eenie-meenie-miny-moe in my head, and opened my mouth to say—

"What do you think you're doing?" An angry male voice cut into my process.

I looked up to see Manny stalking out of the darkness toward us. "Get off my car!"

Once he was close enough, he saw who I was.

"Di? Is that you?" Rhetorical questions. Then, he said. "That's my car."

"It is?" I asked.

Manny turned his attention to Eagle. "You!" he said. "Are you following me again?"

"No, man." Eagle raised both hands in surrender. "Kats and I are just trying to figure out what to do with our evening."

It wasn't entirely a lie.

He continued, "C'mon, Kats. Let's get out of this guy's way." He put an arm around my waist and started directing me back down the alley.

I almost went along, but then I didn't. It wasn't a conscious thought. I just slipped out of Eagle's hold and turned back, walking quickly to rejoin Manny. I felt personally offended that he might be involved in the kidnapping—my first crush. No, I couldn't just let it go.

Manny was in the process of opening his car door.

I said, "Manchester Ortiz, you're up to no good. Why have you been skulking around? I saw you the night of the fire. You were at the house."

Eagle groaned behind me, and Manny turned to face me, chin lifted. "Is that so? You must have good eyesight, if you saw me there. Or an impressive imagination."

"It was you. There's a video. Won't be long, and the police'll be breaking your door down."

"This is none of your business." Manny crossed his arms on his chest and gave me a menacing look. "You should keep your nose to yourself."

"It is my business if you've got Anthony and are trying to get a ransom for him. My mom is delivering that ransom, and so help me god, if you hurt her in any way…"

Behind me, Eagle went so silent that I could hear the wheels turning in his head.

Manny looked furious. "I didn't realize you were such an idiot, Di. Is that what you think?"

A new fire burned up the rims of my ears. "What have you done, Manny? Why were you there that night?"

For an excruciating minute, Manny just glared at me. Then, when I thought he was about to pull a gun and shoot us, he said, "It was a prank."

"Aha! So you do have Anthony!"

"No." Manny shook his head, posture relaxing. "I have no idea what happened to Anthony. I've been taking mementos, knickknacks, and old costume jewelry that belonged to my parents and burying them in the yard. I wanted to see if Gregorio noticed they were missing."

"You buried them? Why?"

"Because it was cathartic, burying all the useless old crap that mattered to them."

"Like they buried you?"

"What?"

"The inheritance. I know you got none of it."

"Again, I'll point out that this is none of your business."

I put my hands firmly on my hips. "Is that why you were in the pawn shop just now. Selling them? That's theft, Manny."

"I wasn't selling them." Manny rubbed his hands over his face. "I had every intention of using them as a scavenger hunt one day, but someone has been digging them up and stealing them. I've been searching local pawn shops to see if I can find them."

"What? You expect me to believe that?"

"Yeah. Because it's true. I'm neither a thief nor a kidnapper. Now, what's this about a ransom and Mrs. Kats delivering it?"

Coming from his mouth, I understood why I wasn't supposed to tell anyone. "Oh, yeah. About that. You should talk to your brother. He knows more about what's going on than I do. Whatever you do, don't tell the police. Gotta run!" I turned and literally ran down the alley, flying past Eagle, who followed me with his eyes.

I got to Eagle's car and had to wait for him to catch up. He had the keys. He walked casually toward me, his face lifted with an expression of wry surprise.

"There's a ransom?" he said before unlocking the car.

"Didn't I mention that?"

"You did not."

I sighed with reluctance. "Let's get in, and I'll tell you about it." I kept one eye on the alley in case Manny backed out. I didn't want to see him again. Moreso, I didn't want him to see me seeing him again.

Eagle clicked the button on the remote, and the car doors all unlocked.

I pulled the door open and dropped into the seat.

Taking his sweet time, Eagle got in behind the wheel. He twisted to face me and said, "Start talking."

My cellphone buzzed. To stall, I looked down at it, half-expecting it to be Mom. It wasn't.

Pamela Garrett was calling me.

I lifted an index finger toward Eagle then answered. "Hello, Mrs. Garrett. How's Hawaii?"

" Hello, Diana, dear. Hawaii is magickal in all ways. As a matter of fact, my husband and I are on our way to a dinner show, so I can't talk long. I'm trying to reach your mother. Is she with you?"

"No, ma'am. She's at your place, I believe."

"Well. She isn't answering her phone."

"Can I give her a message?"

"Yes, please. My son Donald needs to grab some paperwork from the office at the house. Our trip is almost over, and he's decided not to join us after all. The truth is that we're having such a wonderful time, we barely even noticed his absence. Can you please let your mother know to expect him?"

"I will. You enjoy your dinner show." I met Eagle's gaze and saw the impatience there. I looked away.

"Thank you, dear. Have a good night."

"You too."

"Well?" Eagle prompted.

"That was the lady my mom's catsitting for. She wanted me to deliver a message."

Mom was probably not answering Pamela because she was expecting an important call from the kidnapper. She didn't like multi-tasking.

Eagle was unrelenting. "That's not what I meant."

"Hold on," I said and speed-dialed Mom. It rang and rang then went to her messages. For the same reason, she wasn't picking up my call. I left a quick message. "Mom, it's Diana. Pamela just called to let me know that her son will be coming by to grab some things. He doesn't know about the ransom and could mess it up. I'm on my way. I'll try to head him off, if I can."

Saint Eagle displayed great patience. He waited for me to hang up then took my phone from me and held it out of reach. "What is going on?"

I had no choice but to fill him in.

◆◆◆

◆

**Ancestry is myopic.
We all spring from the same source.**

—sign at the Wyrdwood Universalist Church

◆

41

MUSE
Confronts his nemesis.

Did I mention how much I hated that kid? His screaming set my teeth on edge. It was what he did when he wasn't getting his way. His parents usually caved when he did that, especially in public.

While he was throwing his tantrum, I snuck out of my hiding place, crept up behind him, and surgically stuck one claw in the toe of his slipper. It went through smoothly, as I knew it would, and I felt it pierce the sucking sponginess of his flesh.

I was ready when the kid leapt back and kicked out at me. Stupid, fat child. He was no match for me. I'd achieved my goal, which was to interrupt that mind-numbing scream.

"Hey!" Kitty said, bless her. "Don't kick the cat!" She didn't realize I'd just done a North Vietnamese torture technique on him. "Anthony," she said with a new sharpness in her voice. "I'll hold off on calling your folks, for now. But, you need to settle down."

I skirted wide around the kid and went to rub Kitty's ankles. She'd earned some positive reinforcement.

Apparently, she thought I did too. She bent to pet my head as she said, "I have some questions for you, if that's okay?"

Anthony eyed me with the kind of hatred you reserve for your nemesis, and I met his gaze full on.

Kitty diverted his attention back to her. "When did you get here?"

The kid shrugged.

"Okay, so what happened the night of the fire? How did it get started?"

Anthony's gaze dropped, and he lost some of his hiss. "I don't know."

Kitty sat down on the floor to be closer to his level—and mine. "You must have some idea."

"I didn't do anything."

"I'm not saying you did, honey. I just want to know what happened. I know the lights went out. Did you do that?"

"No. They just did. I tried to get them back on, but I couldn't. So, I lit a candle."

"Was someone else there? Did someone come in the house?"

Anthony nodded. "I think it was a robber. It was dark. I thought maybe it was Sherry, but it wasn't. I heard 'em coming, so I ran. The candle fell over. I think the robber bumped it. It wasn't my fault."

"I understand. So you came here to hide?"

"Yeah."

"And you've been here ever since?"

"Yeah."

"You weren't kidnapped?"

"I don't think so." Anthony's confusion resembled disgust.

"I think you would know if you had been."

"Okay."

"Are you hurt anywhere?"

"No."

"Are you hungry?"

"Yeah." That got him bright-eyed. The kid was always hungry.

"C'mon." Kitty got to her feet. "Let's go upstairs. It's warmer up there, and I can make you a sandwich. Then, we can call your folks."

I barely had time to react before Anthony opened his maw and let out another great caterwaul.

Kitty cringed.

The scream hid the sound of heavy footfalls on the floor overhead, to everyone but me. I looked up. My instincts fired off. Danger. Predator. My tail puffed up. My claws came out. I waited, ready to fight or dart back into hiding at the slightest threat.

"Stop, stop, stop," Kitty was pleading with the kid.

"I don't want to call my parents," Anthony said. His bratty tone was barely more endurable than the scream.

Then, footfalls sounded overhead.

Kitty looked up.

The kid heard them a few seconds later. "Who's that?" he sneered, too loudly.

"Shhhh." Kitty put her finger to her lips.

"You can't make me go back!" the kid shouted.

"Quiet!" Kitty crept toward the stairs.

The intruder above stopped at the basement door.

Just as Kitty put her foot on the bottom stair, the door opened at the top.

My body hunkered down closer to the floor. Instinct.

A man stood there. The kitchen light backlit him, turning him into a silhouette. He was wearing a mask on his head, a balaclava.

For several seconds, everyone froze. Including me. We all needed a moment to process the situation.

The man was the first to speak. He said, "Where's the money?"

Kitty didn't reply. I could practically read her thoughts. Why should I pay you? I have the kid. Who are you? Will you hurt us? She couldn't get past all those questions to answer him.

So, he said with more menace, "Where's the money?"

Fumbling in her pocket, Kitty searched for her phone.

She'd left it on the counter upstairs, of course.

"Lady," the man said, "Just tell me where the money is, or you'll both regret it."

I wondered if he meant me and her? Or the kid and her? Probably the latter, I decided.

Kitty found her voice. "You lied. You didn't have him this whole time."

"Yeah, so? I saw an opportunity and I took it. I had nothing to lose. I still don't." He asked again for the money, and this time, he dropped some expletives to emphasize how serious he was. "The Ortizes have more money than they know what to do with. It's time they shared a little."

I couldn't disagree with that. The Ortizes were money magnets—and magnates. They would pass all that family wealth and poison down to their spoiled brat.

"Tell me where it is, and I'll get out of here."

"Donny Garrett, is that you?"

Uh oh. I stared at Kitty, trying to get her to back off with my mind-vibes. Stop. Don't poke the dog! She'd nailed the dog's identity, but by doing so, she'd cornered him.

"Tell me!" More cussing followed, and a not-too-nice string of name-calling. He was getting desperate and frustrated.

Kitty gasped. "It's behind the recliner!"

The man glanced over his shoulder toward the recliner. "If you're lying to me..." He backed up and slammed the basement door shut. After a beat, his footfalls crossed heavily back across the ceiling.

We stood still, listening, as he moved around and finally went to the front door.

The kid asked, "Can we eat now?"

"Yes," Kitty replied and climbed the stairs. She tried the knob, but it wouldn't turn. She jiggled it. She jerked and pushed it. She growled in frustration.

The man had locked us in.

Kitty sat down on the top stair, scratching her forehead. "I guess we have to wait for someone to come find us."

The kid cursed like an adult. "I'm starving!"

"Eat your snacks," Kitty suggested.

"I'm tired of them! This is so unfair!" Anthony started knocking things off shelves, throwing a tantrum.

I lay down on the far side of the basement, never once turning my back on him.

It came as the slightest tickle to my nose. I recognized it immediately, having been overwhelmed by it for days. Smoke. Burning. Danger.

I leapt to my feet and ran up the stairs. I stretched against Kitty's leg and meowed loudly. I tried hard to get her to read my thoughts, but she was resistant. Even if she heard them, she didn't immediately recognize them for what they were.

Kitty took a deep breath through her nose and frowned. Her hand had risen to pet me, but it went still on my back. Realization dawned on her.

"Fire. The house is on fire. Oh my god!" She pushed up to her feet. "Anthony, we have to..."

The kid was nowhere in sight.

◆

Time erodes even the highest mountains.

*—from a placemat at Our Pad,
a Thai/Chinese/American restaurant*

◆

42

DIANA
Can't find Kitty.

Eagle and I were too late. By the time we got to the Garrett's, there was no sign of Pamela's son, and the ransom exchange appeared to have happened. The Ortiz boy came around the corner of the house at a run then stopped and stood there staring up at it.

At first, I didn't recognize him.

Eagle asked, "Isn't that...Anthony Ortiz?" He slowed and pulled toward the curb to park.

I looked more closely. "Yeah. I think so. Wow."

"What's he doing?"

"I don't know." I followed the boy's gaze to the house and saw firelight glinting off the windows on the first floor. My heart leapt into my throat.

"Fire!" I jumped out of Eagle's car before he'd even come to a complete stop. I heard him call, "Diana, wait!" and ignored him.

I sprinted across the lawn to the Ortiz boy and grabbed him by the shoulders. "What happened? Where's my mom?"

He looked terrified. Not of the fire, but of me. He stumbled back so abruptly that he fell on his ass.

"Ant'ony!" A woman called his name, and the boy looked toward her. He abruptly broke into tears and scrambled to his feet. He ran across the lawn toward Badahlia Ortiz, his mother. She ran toward him as well. Under other circumstances, it would have been a beautiful reunion, but I had no time for that.

Eagle joined me. He had his phone to his ear, talking to 911 with an urgency in his voice that I hadn't thought possible. He put a hand on my wrist, presumably to keep me from rushing into the burning building. That restraint probably saved my life.

"Where's my mom?" I asked him.

His reply didn't comfort me. "The fire department is on the way."

◆◆◆

43

MUSE
Tries to save Kitty.

Iknew exactly where the kid had gone. He'd wasted no time at all in fleeing. I hadn't seen him go, but I'd heard him climb out the window at the back of the basement. Little jerk had left us there to be incinerated. That's right, kid. Save yourself.

Kitty was searching for him, calling out his name, and looking in cubbyholes way too small for his Holy Chunkiness to fit into.

She searched the basement. To no avail. The kid had already skedaddled.

The smoke took on a bitter, acid edge. It reminded me of plastic and other man-made abominations. My instincts told me it was toxic.

I went to the window, and—I must confess—the thought did occur to me to save myself. I overcame that urge. A noble king-in-exile does not leave his subjects behind. Instead, I yowled loud enough to save my soul.

Kitty didn't immediately stop her search for the kid. Her voice had grown panicky, and she coughed every third or fourth word. The last coughing fit ended with her gagging. If she stayed in there any longer, she'd pass out and might never leave the building alive.

Hysterical, Kitty shouted, "Anthony, where are you?"

I stuck my nose out the window, took a deep breath, and yowled again. I put every ounce of fear and determination I had into that cry, stared at her intently, and used my mind to send a message of "Come here!"

That got her attention. Kitty made her way toward me. She wiped tears from her eyes and saw the window.

"Oh!" she cried in surprise. "Did Anthony go out that way?"

I put my paw on the sill.

She crawled up on the crates, as clumsy as a kitten, and pushed open the window. It swung upward and outward. Then, she put her hand on my bottom and shoved me out.

I went willingly then turned to watch her.

People were shouting on the lawn at the front of the house.

I stayed with Kitty.

"Anthony better be out here," she said. "Oh my god. He better be."

She clenched her jaw and started to squeeze out, but her chest got stuck. Her breasts. She pushed and pulled them, trying to maneuver out the window. She was fluffy and fat, but she had to get out. I dropped my own chest to the ground, butt in the air, and encouraged her onward.

I couldn't believe it when she abruptly stopped trying and her eyes grew wide. My first thought was that someone had grabbed her by the foot.

"Greta!" she hissed. "Oh my god, Greta!"

Before I could produce an objection, she'd gone back in. And to add insult to injury, she closed and locked the window.

I was left staring in through the glass, watching her cross back toward the stairs. I was powerless to help her.

◆◆◆

◆

There are only two ways to live your life.
One is as though nothing is a miracle.
The other is as though everything is a miracle.

—Albert Einstein

◆

44

KITTY
Searches for Greta.

My heart hurt, both from the smoke and from realizing I'd almost abandoned Greta to a fiery fate. I had no idea whether I could find her or not, but I had to try. She was my responsibility.

The air had grown acrid.

I had to get that door open. I remembered seeing tools, a pile of tools, in the corner. So, I started there and found a shovel, the kind with the pointed tip. It would have to do. I carried it up the stairs with me.

The higher I went, the thicker the smoke, and before long, I was struggling to breathe without coughing. I pulled the neck of my shirt up over my mouth and nose, but it kept sliding down. I needed my hands to wield the shovel.

I shoved the blade in where the door met the jamb and tried to lever the door open. The shovel slipped. I tried again, and it slipped out again. One more time, I pulled on the shovel with all my weight. When it slipped out, I was thrown off-balance and hovered over the open staircase—my life passing before my eyes. I saw mostly Diana, as an infant, a baby, a toddler, a grade-schooler, a teen, and a young woman. My last thoughts would have been of her, but my hand landed on the railing. I latched onto it and saved myself from a deadly fall.

Nevertheless, the shovel tumbled down the stairs with a loud clatter.

A coughing fit overcame me. Once it was over, I went

back down the stairs, stepped over the shovel, and searched for a better tool. I found a hammer in the tool pile. It had heft and felt sturdy in my hands. As quickly as I could manage, I hurried back up the stairs, keeping one hand on the railing to steady myself. My legs grew more wobbly with each passing moment.

The hammer was no more effective at prying open the door than the shovel had been. I imagined Greta upstairs, hiding somewhere, terrified, and my heart nearly broke. No matter how hard I tried, I couldn't pry the door open.

Frustrated and angry, I swung the hammer at the door with a growling scream. It hurt my throat, but the hammer cracked the wood in the panel. Hope filled me. I swung again and again, breaking a hole in the wood. Smoke leaked out of it, but I felt no heat. I hoped the fire was focused, for the moment, in the living room.

I made a hole big enough to reach out and unlock the door. It swung open.

Dropping to my hands and knees, I left the hammer behind and crawled into the kitchen. I'd been right. The fire was consuming the living room. It crawled up the walls and curtains. Even the front door was completely blocked by the flames.

"Greta! C'mere, honey! Greta baby. C'mere, Greta!" I had no idea where she would be, so I listened. My hope was that she would meow. I was so afraid she'd gone upstairs to hide. Following her would have been a suicide mission.

The fire had a voice too, one that filled me with terror.

I kept repeating Greta's name, trying to keep the panic out of my voice. I didn't want her to be afraid of me. "Greta!"

Then I saw her, hiding behind the dining table leg. Her spot. I locked eyes with her and made a gesture to summon her to me. I blinked slowly. I could see her indecision. She looked back and forth between the living room and me.

I crawled toward her. "C'mon, kitten. Come to me. We

need to get out of here. Please." When I got close enough, I reached out and grabbed her by the scruff. She'd been just about to panic, I could tell. I latched onto her, and I wasn't about to let her go. I pulled her in against my body and felt her dig every one of her claws into me.

"Good girl," I rasped. "You hang on tight."

The heat of the fire warmed my cheeks. The smoke burned my eyes.

I got to my feet as quickly as I could and rushed back to the basement stairs. That was where the only safe exit was.

I kept coughing, and my eyes swam with tears. I could barely see the stairs. I felt my way down one step at a time and crossed the basement to the window. When I got there, a little black face with wide eyes was staring in at me. I've never been so happy to see anyone in my whole life.

I climbed up to where I could reach the lock and pushed open the window.

"Go on, Greta. Go out." I pulled her off me one claw at a time and lifted her toward the window. She didn't need to be told twice.

Climbing out after her, I scraped my boobs. I managed to get them through, but my hips were a different story. I was stuck.

"Help!" I called, though it came out as a ragged croak rather than an actual shout. I wiggled and squirmed. I thought I could inch my way through, but then my feet came up off the crates, and I had no way to push myself from behind.

Muse licked my face.

"Not now, kitten," I said, trying to keep him from licking my eyes.

It was no use. I was stuck.

I was desperate. Instinct kicked in. I needed out. I needed to *not* die. I needed...magick. It coiled in my center and rose up through my gorge. At first, I thought I was going to throw up, but instead, I shrunk inward like a wave flowing out to sea. That and one determined push with my hands were enough that I slid through the window and landed on the grass outside. A second later, the wave rolled back in, refilling me. And that time, I did puke.

Shortly thereafter, I felt hands helping me up and away from the building. We didn't go far. I didn't have the strength. The hands lowered me back down to the lawn, and I sat cross-legged.

Familiar arms wrapped around me. I heard Diana crying next to my ear.

I tried to comfort her. "It's—" A coughing fit interrupted me. Someone put a mask on my face, oxygen, and its cold was deeply comforting.

A warm body crawled into my lap. At first, I thought it was Muse, but when I blinked back the tears, I saw it was Greta. She lay there shaking, head buried against my belly.

◆◆◆

45

DIANA

Is ambulance chasing.

The paramedics peeled me off Mom, and I reluctantly backed off. They wrapped her in a blanket and put an oxygen mask on her.

Flashing lights cast a strobe effect on the dark neighborhood, blue and lots of red. The fire truck was in position to spray water upon the house. Police and Rescue vehicles were blocking the road.

I felt the emotional aftermath swell inside me. I was about to cry. When I turned to walk away though, I ran square into a solid chest—Eagle. There was no delaying the tears. Great sobs shook my body, and Eagle held me against himself to keep me from collapsing. All I could think about was how close I'd come to losing her.

"Did you...Anthony?" Mom was trying to speak, but the paramedics were discouraging it.

"Anthony?" she tried again, waving her hands frantically.

"He's okay," replied a rich, masculine voice. "Kitten, he got out. Don't worry." It was the fire chief, calling my mom 'Kitten.' Was I hallucinating?

I wrangled my breakdown, getting it under control, wiping my eyes, and reluctantly pushing away from Eagle. "Thanks," I mumbled. I saw the wet spot on his shirt. "Sorry."

"No problem," was all he replied. He released me but kept a light touch on my shoulder. It was probably for the best. I was shaking in the aftermath of the adrenaline, and there was no guarantee I wouldn't lose it again.

"Take good care of her," the chief said. "She's precious cargo." He meant my mom.

The paramedics replied in the affirmative.

"My hero," whispered Mom. It was impossible to tell whether she was being sarcastic or not.

"You okay?" asked a different male voice. Nick. I turned to meet his gaze. He was not talking to Mom. He was talking to me.

"Yeah, Boss. I'm okay."

He nodded, and the crease in his forehead eased a bit. Gently, he approached Mom and squatted down beside her. "Mrs. Kats. Was it the kidnapper?"

I was surprised he knew about that.

As if reading my thoughts, he said to Mom, "Mr and Mrs Ortiz told me what's happening. We need to find whoever did this. Do you know who it was?"

Mom nodded. She pulled her mask aside and croaked two words, obviously pained by speaking. "Donny Garrett."

"Donald?" asked Nick in surprise. "You're sure?"

Mom nodded again. The paramedic put her mask back on her.

After that, Nick was in motion. No more gentleness. He rose and strode across the lawn, talking firmly into his radio. He called for an APB on Donald Garrett.

The ambulance arrived, and they came with a stretcher to take Mom to the hospital. She tried to refuse, but they weren't taking 'no' for an answer.

"Di!" Mom called, her voice husky.

"Yeah, Mom." I hurried to her side. "I'm here. What do you need?"

"Take Greta." She lifted the cat from her lap. "Take her home."

"I can't. I'm going to the hospital with you."

"No. Please. Take...Greta." She was getting upset.

"Okay," I said. I took the traumatized cat from her. "I will. Then, I'm coming to the hospital. I'll be there soon."

It took me a moment to realize that the cat I was holding had buried her head in the crook of my arm and was clinging to me. My heart went out to her. "It's okay, honey," I said. "You're going to be okay." I sounded so much like my mother, and for the first time, it didn't bother me.

I followed the stretcher to the ambulance, walking past a line of neighbors all gawping at the spectacle. They called out well-wishes to Mom as she went by, and Mom waved weakly at them.

I'd known those neighbors all my life. They'd oohed and ahhed at my Halloween costumes when I was trick-or-treating. They'd bought lemonade at my lemonade stand. They'd patched up my scraped knee when I fell on my rollerskates. They'd given me cookies and milk—just because. In that moment, I loved them all more than I could have expressed.

Rose Silva stepped forward and gave me a quick side hug as I went by.

Mike Cook patted my shoulder, the one that wasn't still occupied by Eagle's hand.

My tears started up again, and I cried into Greta's fur all the way home in Eagle's car.

"It's okay, honey," I whispered, unsure of whether I was talking to Greta or myself.

◆◆◆

◆

**When Rome burned,
the emperor's cats still
expected to be fed on time.**

—Seanan McGuire

◆

46

MUSE
Is too tired to give a poop.

I ran after Diana. Relief filled me when the car stopped at the house. Our house. Our home. My home. I was exhausted and starving. I wanted warmth, comfort, and a full belly. Kitty's well-being was out of my control. The doctors had taken over. It was time to address the needs of His Majesty Muse.

I was so tired that I didn't even care that Diana brought Greta inside and put her in my bed. First stop: food and water. Then nap.

After eating, I sat in a pool of darkness, licking my whiskers and paws, and it occurred to me just how close we'd all come to dying. Well, not me, since I'm immortal. The others, however, were not. Gratitude overwhelmed me. I'd have been devastated if Kitty had died. The emotion was too intense.

In my weakened state, I crawled into my bed with Greta. She was asleep—a blessing. I applied a few tentative licks to her head and, when she didn't react with claws or teeth, I cleaned her. She tasted like smoke and fear. It was unpleasant and yet satisfying to remove. By the time I curled up beside her, lending my body warmth to hers, she was mine.

◆◆◆

◆

Let's pretend I can't see you.

— bumper sticker

◆

47

MUSE
Ponders the nature of change.

Stupid firefighters. They found my stash. It didn't take them long to figure out the objects belonged to the Ortizes. From what I heard, they blamed the young Garrett for the theft and tried to work that into his motive for kidnapping. Of course, Manny the Little Man didn't correct them. He got off scot-free. And I lost my treasure. I was not amused.

In one regard, I came out on top. I never saw the Ortizes again. That kid was relegated to a distant, unpleasant memory. I shouldn't have been surprised that they never asked for me back, but I will admit that it hurt my feelings. Not that I wanted to go back to them. I definitely did not. However, it would have been nice if they'd cared enough to fight for me. Ah well. Such is the life of a vagabond king.

Mini-Mimi—the hairball on sticks—would probably never change, and I'd resigned myself to the fact that she annoyed the snot out of me. Someday—oh yes, someday—I would have my moment. When that happened, she would be banished from my presence. For the nonce, I toyed with her as one would toy with a mouse. She was almost as smart as a tiny rodent, so it amused me. My favorite game was jumping out at her when she least expected it. She never saw me coming, and she got in trouble for barking afterward. It was ambrosia.

Greta stayed with us for a while. Her people needed time to reestablish a home, and they were paying Kitty to take care of her. Greta was not the head of a household anymore, but I had shown her that I could be a benevolent lord and master. She humored me. I sometimes caught her thinking about ways to reassert her dominance, but nope. I was not about to allow that.

I tolerated her presence. The baths and naps we shared were for my benefit, not hers. Honest.

◆◆◆

48

DIANA
Wraps up.

The sheriff caught up with Donald Garrett at the airport. He'd been caught attempting to fly to Hawaii with the ticket he'd failed to use during his parents' vacation. He wasn't too bright, which would explain why his business was floundering. He hadn't even bothered to move the money to a new suitcase. He'd gone to the airport with it in hand.

When the deputies brought him, handcuffed, into the station, he was proclaiming loudly that he hadn't actually kidnapped anyone, and he was planning to pay back the money. As if that made all the difference in the world to his guilt or innocence.

I had to put up with Nick crowing over the win for a whole day. As if he'd been responsible for the arrest. I just sat back and laughed at him behind my hand.

My first paycheck, as it turned out, was *not* from the sheriff's department, but from Eagle—and it was a big one. I was shocked until I realized he was buttering me up. My little displays of "magick" had impressed him. Those zeros made it hard to say no, and that was why he did it.

Nevertheless, I was not ready to give up my chichi job with the police. Not yet. I told Eagle I'd help him part-time.

Eagle told *me* he'd get me to go full-time within six months.

I welcomed the challenge.

Speaking of challenges, my lawyer, Divana Smart, delivered a copy of the divorce papers. I left them on the cardboard box beside my bed. I haven't been able to bring myself to read them yet, much less sign them. It's too much like giving up, like losing at the game of Life. Truth is, I *have* lost, but that doesn't mean I'm ready to fully concede. Denial isn't just a river in Egypt, as they say. Baby steps. I was sure my darling husband would do something that would make me sign them in a fit of rage. It was only a matter of time.

Mom spent a couple days in the hospital. They wanted her to stay in bed for another day or two, but she was incapable of sitting still. She was up and at 'em the very next morning.

"I have responsibilities," she said. She got a few new catsitting clients as word spread of the lengths to which she would go in order to save a cat. She was the Wyrdwood North Hero of the Week. People sent flowers, candy, balloons, cards, and home-baked goods. It was magickal to watch her blush and flounder in the face of so much attention and praise. Once I got over being embarrassed for her, the outpouring of love did my heart good.

On top of all that, a check arrived from the Ortizes, and I thought she was going to faint.

◆◆◆

49

KITTY
Moves on to a new adventure.

I didn't faint. I cried. The reward from the Ortizes arrived by special messenger in the form of a cashier's check. It was everything they'd promised. I cried because I'd be able to pay my back mortgage and have enough left over to cover the next month's mortgage as well. For the moment, I was saved. My house was still my own.

Exactly three days after I paid the overdue amount, my doorbell rang. I opened the door to discover the bitter bow-tied man standing on my front stoop. He must have needed the jaws of life to unclench his...jaw. I'd rarely seen anyone so angry in my life.

He didn't even wait for me to greet him but started in on a tirade about how "This isn't over, Kats. You think you've won, but I'm playing the long game. Your family will pay for what you've done to mine. I curse you, do you hear me? I curse you and all those who are your blood. Cursed! You are cursed!" He waved his fingers around in jiggly swoops.

I slammed the door in his face. From beyond it, I heard, "Cursed!"

Shaking my head, I went back to doing the dishes and put him out of my mind.

Not an hour later, I got a call from an old friend. I hadn't seen Martha Fishgiven for years. She and her husband Harold owned a home on the same lake where Bob and I used to rent a cabin each summer. They were about a decade older than us, and over the years, we'd become friends. They'd have us over for dinner at least once per summer, and we'd invite them to the cabin for a barbecue. Bob and Harold often fished together. It had become a tradition.

Martha had been one of the first to call and offer condolences after Bob died. Her friendship meant a lot.

"Hello? Martha?"

"Why, yes, dear! How lovely to hear your voice." Martha was British by birth and accent, and so she spoke like that. It was charming.

"Yours too. How are you doing?" I leaned against the kitchen counter and focused on the call.

"I'm afraid I have some bad news. My Harold has come to a sticky end."

"Oh. That sounds awful." I had no idea what she meant.

"Yes, it rather is. He was murdered the night before last. I need to accompany him to his family estate where he will be buried."

Suddenly, I understood. "Oh no!" My new response rose to the occasion. "Martha, I'm so sorry! He was murdered?" The newly awakening detective in me sat up and took notice.

"So the police tell me. They say he was poisoned."

"By whom?"

"We don't know. Maybe his caretaker? I was in London, you see, visiting my mother who is also quite ill. I'm fortunate that it wasn't I who found him. I keep imagining walking in the door with my bags and stumbling over his body."

"Oh, goodness. I'm so glad *that* didn't happen."

"Yes, you see how hard it's been on me? Now, I have to return to my mother's side. She has gone downhill, and I don't expect her to pull out this time either. Which brings me to why I'm calling. I wonder if I could ask you for a huge favor?"

"Of course, anything."

"I need someone to come and house-sit for a while. I

have my cats, you see, and they need someone to care for them. Would you be available?"

"I'll make myself available," I told her, sorting through my current commitments in my head. "It'll take me a few days to get there. I'll need to clear my calendar." I pushed off the counter and went into my office.

"It's too much bother, isn't it? I shouldn't have called." I could hear the growing panic in her voice.

"Martha, no. It's no problem. I just have to make arrangements. How long do you think you'll be gone?" My calendar was taped to the wall.

"A week? Maybe two? Unfortunately, there's no set timeline for when my mother will no longer need me."

"I think I can drive up day after tomorrow. Will that be soon enough?"

"Oh, yes. That would be perfect. Thank you so much, love. Your kindness will come back to you tenfold."

I didn't know what to say to that, so I said nothing.

She continued. "I must go. I have an appointment with the travel agent to arrange a flight for Harold and myself. And please, dear, bring Diana, if you wish."

"Oh, she's working now. I doubt she can get the time off."

"Brava! A real career girl. Well, toodles. I'll see you when you get here."

"I'll call if I run into any snags."

"No snags allowed," Martha said with a ghost of a chuckle.

♦♦♦

50

MUSE
Speaks too soon.

One day, in the distant future, I will look back on that era as one of the best of my life. I was content, to say the least. I'd found my new castle, where they appreciated me. We'd survived two fires and had gotten rid of the Ortiz menaces forever. Greta had come around to my charms, and I'd discovered I liked how she smelled, after all. It wasn't perfect, but it was good. Real good.

The drama and danger were behind us, at last.

Right?

◆◆◆

Post Mortem

MAYOR VIOLET BAGLEY
Files her notes.

Case resolved. Fire Chief Elias Kariuki ruled that the fire at the Ortiz residence was an accident with no casualties. The kidnapping turned out to be fraudulent. The perpetrator (Donald Garrett) was captured and is facing trial by his peers for felony extortion.

Witness depositions proceeded without incident. The primary witnesses were debriefed (with informed consent) under the influence of a bareface spell, as required by Wyrdwood law.

Of those interviewed, King Muse interested me the most. I knew he'd been given sanctuary in Wyrdwood and that he'd been here since long before my birth, but I didn't realize how active he was. He has a mischievous side, and I don't ever want to go head-to-head with him. While I'm confident I'd come out on top, I also know I'd walk away with scars.

Also of note is Kitty Kats. She stands at a critical stage in her evolution. Even she's not aware of it. Her mother wasn't around long enough to teach her about her own kin—the dakini. These beings tend to come into their powers as crones. It's still TBD how powerful she will be. Her husband (Robert "Bob" Kats) died, so perhaps her daughter will step up and give Mrs. Kats the stability she needs to navigate the Change.

The daughter, Diana Kats, may keep me busy. She started proceedings to kick her husband (Kyle Butts) to the curb, and that gives me hope for her. However, she has a reckless streak, much like her father did. I'll keep half an eye on her—for her own good.

For that matter, I'll be monitoring all three of them.

[End of incident report, Ortiz fire and extortion, filed by Violet Bagley, Mayor, Wyrdwood, Oregon.]

Thanks for Reading

WW301222

That concludes *The Catsitter's Conundrum*, though Kitty, Diana, and Muse will be back in a new adventure.

Join our growing community by signing up for the Wyrdwood email list at the link below. We'll send instructions for how to connect with other magickal readers just like you.

If you enjoyed this story, please take a moment to give it a review wherever you purchased it. It's the kindest gift you can give the authors you love and who love you back (like me!).

Read more. A Wyrdwood novella, titled "Charlie Darwin, Or The Trine Of 1809," is available as a free download at:

https://www.angelmccoy.com/wyrdwood-home/

Visit Wyrdwood

Know anyone you think would like this story?
Please let them know about it!
They'll be thankful you did and so will I.

◆◆◆

Angel Leigh McCoy

I believe in magick. Whether you believe or not is up to you. Wyrdwood is the town I wish I lived in, and its residents are the people I wish were friends and enemies.

Life can be so dark, sad, and terrifying—for us all. Sometimes it's easy to forget the things that save us from that. I hope these books will remind you that—even in our darkest hours—there is hope, light, love, and laughter.

About me: I'm the spark of creative force behind the darkly fanciful Wyrdwood project and the epic Dire Multiverse.

I'm an award-winning video game writer, having worked on "CONTROL," IGN's Game of the Year 2019. Prior to that, I spent twenty years weaving intricate tales for millions of fans of *Guild Wars 2* and *White Wolf's World of Darkness*.

After two decades in the big city of Seattle, I've settled down in a small town not unlike Wyrdwood. Life is an adventure—daily.

◆◆◆

Copyright

The Catsitter's Conundrum

https://angelmccoy.com/wyrdwood-home

♦♦♦

9 781950 427161